LEVON'S RUN

A VIGILANTE JUSTICE THRILLER BOOK 4

CHUCK DIXON

ROUGH EDGES PRESS

Published in the United States by Wolfpack Publishing, Las Vegas

Rough Edges Press
An Imprint of Wolfpack Publishing
5130 S. Fort Apache Rd. 215-380
Las Vegas, NV 89148
roughedgespress.com

Paperback ISBN 978-1-68549-039-3
eBook ISBN 978-1-68549-029-4

LEVON'S RUN

1

Bando blamed his bitch of a girlfriend for everything.

If his bitch of a girlfriend didn't spend all the money he gave her for their kid.

If his bitch of a girlfriend didn't keep bitching about visiting her mother in Miami. Bitched that Connecticut in February was too damn cold. Only she didn't have any money because she spent every dime he gave her for the kid.

If his bitch of girlfriend could just learn to budget he wouldn't have had to rob that Xtra Mart.

If he hadn't used her car to rob the Xtra Mart.

If the bitch hadn't told the cops he borrowed the car.

If the bitch didn't tell them where to find him.

It was all his bitch of girlfriend's fault that he was locked up in Middletown City Jail, a guest of the county.

Only good part of all of it was that the cops got all the money.

His bitch of a girlfriend wouldn't be visiting her mother in Miami.

2

"Notice something about these bills?" said the guy from Westbrook Barracks.

"They counterfeit? We thought they might be fake. You never see anything bigger than a twenty at a place like that," said the Middlesex County deputy. He leaned over to look at the bill held stretched between the gloved hands of the trooper.

"They're old," the trooper said.

"Look new to me," the deputy said.

The county had called in Connecticut State Police CID when they spotted the bills taken in as evidence in a convenience store hold-up. They found Lyle James Bandeaux high as a kite in his apartment just as his girlfriend said he'd be. The money was still in the Xtra Mart bag. The weapon used in the robbery was on the floor by him. Dead bang.

"That's the other thing. Series 1993 but still fresh. They're old but they look new." The trooper flicked the edge of the bill. It was crisp.

"Damn," the deputy said, squinting at General Grant's stern visage.

* * *

Connecticut State CID contacted the Federal Reserve Bank in Boston. The trooper faxed over scans of both sides of both bills. The scans remained on the fax machine tray at the Fed until the following morning. An officer there re-faxed the notice from the trooper to Treasury and the FBI.

Old money, especially old money that is clearly uncirculated, makes Fed Reserve officers put down their coffee mugs, sit up, and take notice. The Fed runs a tight ship. An even tighter ship after millions in bills vanished from the reserve bank in Philadelphia back in the 1970s. Used, torn, soiled or simply filthy currency winds up at the Fed for disposal. Before the thefts, the bills were counted and then incinerated. The systems had holes. Lots of holes. And it didn't take a mastermind to hold a few bills back from the fire and slip them into a pocket. It was an inside job that went on for years; a slow-motion looting of old currency slated to be destroyed; a conspiracy of otherwise honest bean counters who couldn't resist the temptation of slipping away with a few dirty old bills that no one would miss. A few dirty old bills turned into wads and wads of dirty old bills adding up to millions.

The thefts were discovered and the Fed was turned upside down and backwards. Officials were fired. Employees went to jail. A few committed suicide. An embarrassment and a tragedy.

The Fed's entire security protocol was then altered to account for every single bill entering the system. Bills to be destroyed are stamped through by a die upon arrival at the bank. The shape of the die identifies which of the twelve reserve banks has taken in each bill. The money is scanned, counted, re-counted, shredded, bleached and spun to a consistency of cotton candy after which it is bagged, tagged and stored in the depths of each Fed branch. At every step of the way, there are more cameras on all involved than at a celebrity wedding.

Long story short, every bill is important to the Fed. And when a pair of fifties, twenty plus years old, and so mint that the ink still stands raised on the rag stock, the Fed gets curious about where those Grants have been all this time and where they came from.

FBI special agent Bill Marquez thought he knew.

3

Bill needed a decent meal, a long hot shower and twelve hours sleep. He wasn't going to get any of it.

He was attached to an ongoing investigation into a home invasion in the woods of Maine. It was part of a string of violent invasions that occurred over the past month or so ranging from Costa Rica to Thailand to Fiji. The crew involved was on the hunt for a big boodle of cash stolen years before by billionaire conman Corey Blanco. They tortured and murdered Blanco and his wife and kids. Then the same crew went on to systematically burglarize other Blanco properties around the world. They left corpses behind everywhere they went.

The latest happened a little more than twenty-four hours before in a flyspeck town in Maine. There were dead victims scattered everywhere around a lake community. There were terrorized survivors, including a kid in a Bangor hospital getting some fingers sewn back on.

Most of the invasion crew were dead. Six, possibly seven, of the actors died at the hand of someone unknown. Shot, stabbed, and in one case, beaten to death. Witnesses gave up nothing on how any of it went down. They pleaded ignorance or refused to cooperate. Early theories were put forth that the gang turned on each other. They found what they were looking for then went blood simple and began taking one another out until they were all dead. An ouroboros serpent of greed.

Based upon the evidence on the ground around Lake Bellevue, Bill Marquez had another idea.

This gang had never left witnesses at their other break-ins. Up in Maine they killed three innocents but left a woman, her daughter and her son alive. On the prior robberies, millions in cash and valuables were left behind. The operating theory was that these guys were pros searching for a particular item. They were so slick they left behind any loot that might later lead to them. This time there were signs that cash and jewels were taken.

And there was the last man standing. Or, more precisely, driving.

Someone survived the slaughter and made it through the woods to take off in one of two getaway cars stashed on a fire road miles from the primary crime scene.

And then there were the three lake residents unaccounted for. Two were a man and his daughter with identities that proved to be bogus. The man left his truck behind but he and the little girl were nowhere to be found. The cabin they shared showed signs of a break-in but no signs of violence. Then there was a woman, also using a phony name, illegally squatting in a mansion directly opposite the Blanco home. The owners of the house were contacted at their winter residence in the Bahamas. They never heard of their uninvited house guest and had not given anyone permission to stay there. The mystery woman's Mercedes G was gone as well.

Now Bill was sitting in the cramped and stuffy manager's office in the back of an Xtra Mart in New Haven. He was reviewing surveillance video on a pair of monitors. One showed the gas pump island. The other offered a view of the store's counter. The manager was a nervous Egyptian guy eager to help. He leaned over Bill's shoulder, breathing garlic in his ear.

"Your sign says you don't take bills larger than a twenty," Bill said as he moved the mouse to race backward through the footage showing the customers at the counter.

"My cousin Yuri is an idiot. He took the money. I tell him and tell him," the manager groused.

"Why did he take it?"

"I told you. He is an idiot."

"Maybe the guy let him keep the change," Bill offered.

The manager huffed a fresh gust of garlic.

On the monitor, Bill watched the high-speed reverse pantomime of Lyle James Bandeaux holding a gun on the counter man and fleeing the store, a plastic bag containing the contents of the till in hand.

"It would be just before that." The manager waggled a finger at the screen.

"How can you know? You watch this?" Bill said without turning from the whirl of customers gliding up and away from the counter in fast-backwards time.

"We do safe drops every hour. The two bills you

are looking for were still in the register."

Bill shrugged.

"There!" The manager stabbed at the screen.

Bill froze the image.

A big guy, broad shoulders, stood at the counter. Ball cap with a hoodie worn under a heavier winter coat. The hood was up over the ball cap. The man's face, even the shape of his head was concealed. Facial recognition programs were going to be useless. His nose, upper lip and chin were visible. He had a week's growth of facial hair. He was a white guy. Despite a clear HD image that's all the video revealed.

Bill wound back and watched the exchange play out from the start in real time. The guy entered to take a place in line behind a pair of young black teens buying sodas. Once they left, he stepped to the counter. He handed over two bills in a gloved hand. There was an exchange between the man and Yuri, the manager's idiot cousin. The cousin gestured with open hands, head shaking. The customer remained unmoving, hand held out with the two bills stiff between his fingers. Yuri gave in at last and took the bills. The guy turned for the door and left.

"Wait." The manager placed a hand atop Bill's hand working the mouse.

Together they watched Yuri ring up the sale, place the two bills beneath the register drawer. Before closing the drawer, he slipped a couple of bills from the tray and pocketed them.

"Son of a bitch!" the manager hissed, releasing Bill's hand.

Bill checked the time stamp on the video. Less than nine hours ago. He switched to the outside footage and moved back to the same time. He watched the hooded man walk to a Mercedes SUV parked by the gas pump island. The same model as the Mercedes that was missing from Lake Bellevue. The man stood pumping gas. There was someone seated inside the SUV in the passenger seat.

"Does this have a zoom feature?" Bill asked.

The manager pointed to a magnifying glass symbol in a drop-down toolbox atop the screen. Bill moved the cursor to the face visible through the windshield and dialed in. A female face. Shoulder length hair. The image was blurred but Bill could see it was a young girl. The mystery man's daughter, if she was his daughter. The angle didn't allow him to see if there was anyone in the back seat.

He watched the man pump the gas, re-hook the nozzle, re-enter the SUV and drive off frame. Then he wound it back and zoomed in on the license plate. Massachusetts plate. He copied the plate numbers on a slip of paper.

Bill asked the manager to make a disc copy of the footage for him. While he waited for the disc to burn he called the FBI office in Boston. He didn't know anyone there. He'd been assigned to the LA office for the past few years. He put on his "take no shit" voice until he got through to an assistant director of that division.

The manager handed off the disc, still warm from the burner. Bill's cell rang back.

"Marquez."

"We ran that plate. The Mercedes is registered to a Kiera Anne Reeves. Listed residence in Boston."

"Can you get someone over there to lock her down? She's a person of interest in this Lake Bellevue mess."

"We won't have to. Cops in Waltham, Mass have her in custody."

Bill peppered the Boston AD with questions as he ran from the store to his car, the disc in hand.

4

"I'm the victim here. Can we try to remember that?" Kiera Anne said.

"What were you doing in that motel room?" Bill Marquez said. His eyes felt like they were filled with sand. The drive back up to Boston hadn't helped.

"I was on vacation," Kiera Anne said, eyes level across the table in the interrogation room. She lowered her head to speak directly to Bill's smartphone set to record the interview. He noticed a bruise on her chin that she'd tried to cover with makeup. In the harsh overhead light, it took on a yellowish hue.

"The room was registered to a Noah Murray of Galveston, Texas."

"Good old Tex," she sighed.

"In addition to playing rough, good old Tex doesn't exist. Why are you protecting someone who left you duct-taped on the bed for the maid to find?"

"I met a guy in a bar. He took me to his motel. Is that a crime?"

"Motel 6 seems kind of down market for you."

"I like an adventure now and then," she said, covering the Patek Phillipe watch on her left wrist with her right hand. She shook her head to free a strand of blonde hair from over her eye and regarded him with a flat expression.

"Let me tell you what we have, okay? Lay my cards on the table and see if you can explain my hand," Bill said, voice as flat as her gaze.

She shrugged and sat back in her chair, eyes closed and mouth downturned.

"We found you trussed like a Christmas present on a bed in a motel room paid for in suspect cash and registered in the name of a man who never was. We also found a Suburban with Canadian plates parked on the lot. It was rented in Toronto under the same stolen name and account as another Suburban found at the scene of a mass murder up in Maine. And your car, a Mercedes G class, was caught on video at a convenience store down in New Haven driven by an unidentified man in the company of a female minor."

"I told the police here it was stolen," she said. There was a pack of cigarettes on the table. She reached for it and peeled away the cellophane.

He glanced at the sign on the wall that read, This Is A Non-Smoking Facility.

"Do you mind?" she said, eyebrow arched.

Bill shrugged and hit the switch by the door, turning on a room vent. He lit the cigarette for her. She released a blue cloud to the ceiling. She cleared her throat and stifled a cough. Not a regular smoker. She was looking for a distraction for herself. For him.

Her hands were steady, he gave her that. But there was a dew of sweat on her upper lip. Her eyes caught him studying her.

"I saw the report on your car. But that's Waltham

P.D.'s problem. The bureau doesn't do auto theft. Would you like to tell me what you were doing in Maine?" he said, retaking his seat across from her.

"Who said I was in Maine?" She flicked ash onto the floor, elbow cupped in her hand, acting casual as hell.

"Because that's what fits. You were married to Courtland Ray Blanco for five years. Divorced fourteen years ago. We have witnesses placing you in Bellevue, Maine for the past month." That was a lie. The three witnesses they had were giving them squat for now. "Your ex-husband was the target of a gang of international thieves who were working their way around the world burglarizing homes owned by him through holding companies and shell accounts. You just happened to be trespassing in a home with a view of Blanco's house on Lake Bellevue at the same time as that home was invaded."

"And you have proof of that," she said.

"Fingerprints. DNA. Everything you see on TV." Another lie. A white one. He expected a report from the crime scene techs confirming her presence in the house. He suspected she cleaned up after herself but, after weeks in that house, she was bound to have missed something.

"You're arresting me for staying in a house that isn't mine?"

"Criminal trespass is a local cop thing. I'm holding you as a material witness to a federal crime. I also have reason to believe your life might be in danger."

Both eyebrows went up at that. She blinked through a stream of rising smoke. Bill kept his face frozen in the solid, unmovable mask of federal authority. It was easy for him since he decided that he did not like this woman.

"You can do that? That will hold up with a lawyer and all that?"

"If you'd rather, we can make the case that you were an accomplice in the home invasions. Not hard to convince a judge to let us charge you. Judges don't like coincidences. And you picking a house with a view of a potential murder scene belonging to your ex is a lot to take on faith."

She sat up and smeared the half-smoked cigarette on the table top. The charade was over.

"What do you want?" She sighed.

"You can start by telling us all you know about Tex," Bill said.

5

He left the former Mrs. Blanco for a detailed follow-up with a pair of Boston bureau agents. They assured him they'd have a computer composite drawing in a few hours. It would be based on Kiera Reese's description and checked against what they had from the Xtra Mart video.

The bureau booked him into a Holiday Inn Express. He took a long stinging shower then lay on the bed, willing his mind to rest. He gave up after only a few minutes.

Nancy Valdez answered on the third ring after he got through to her extension past the information tree at Treasury. She didn't recognize his voice at first.

"You sound ragged," she said. It was good to hear her voice again.

"I'm not even sure what day it is," he said.

"Well, it's only two in the afternoon and you don't sound drunk, so I assume this is business," she said.

"I feel hungover and I haven't had a sip." He laughed, punchy, then filled her in on the case so far.

"What is this?" she said.

"I was hoping you'd tell me, Nance." He was punchy. He'd never called her Nance before.

"It sounds like someone interrupted the crew in flagrante. An unexpected party crasher."

"You think someone cowboyed them? Robbed from the thieves?"

"One guy? With a crew this experienced? And with a kid in tow?"

"So, what is it? Karma?" He pressed the bridge of his nose between his thumb and index finger to release the tightening knot there. It didn't work.

"Shit, Bill. I hate to say what it looks like," she said.

"What do you see that I'm not?"

"A vigilante."

"This guy Tex is Batman?" he said, sitting up.

"And Robin. Don't forget the little girl," Nancy said.

* * *

His phone buzzed, waking him. He could swear he'd only just closed his eyes. The clock on the nightstand read three hours after he'd last looked at it.

"Marquez," he croaked.

"A message from special agent Brompton, sir," a chirpy voice said.

"Go ahead." The sky he could see through the blinds was deep indigo.

"He's sending a car for you. He says it's wheels up in sixty at Minute Man Air Field."

"Okay, okay." He groaned and broke the connection.

The bureau had assigned them a plane. Someone in DC recognized this case was white hot. Recovering a billion or so in funds bilked from private investors would mean headlines. And a few hundred million for the IRS would make whoever recovered it a hero. Bill wondered who'd end up taking the credit once it all cleared.

Bill hobbled to the shower, an old man at thirty-seven.

The young female agent who greeted him in the lobby introduced herself as Mandy. She was fresh out of Quantico and had blood in her eye for promotion. Was he ever that eager? Tired as he was, he admired her calves under the hem of the regulation length skirt as she led him to the car waiting at the turnaround.

She had hot Starbucks and an icy cold orange juice in the cup holders for him. He would have given to her half his kingdom at that point. He sipped the coffee and held the frosty OJ to his forehead. They took off for the airfield.

"We'll need to punch it to make it to Minute Man by the time Agent Brompton's touched down, sir." She expertly shifted lanes to get them onto the right on-ramp for Stow.

Bill balanced the cup to keep the scalding liquid from sloshing from the sip hole onto his pant leg.

"Where's he coming from?" Bill said, eying the inch wide gap between their right fender and the back of a JB Hunt truck they were passing at seventy.

"Bangor. Things have come to a boil. The bureau authorized a Gulfstream. Ever been?" She beamed at the thought, eyes, thank God, locked on the road ahead.

"I haven't."

"Some of them are unbelievable. Seized through

zero tolerance. I was on one last year that belonged to a Sinaloa cartel member. It had a hot tub. A hot tub!"

"There's been a development then?" The coffee was restarting his heart and mind.

"They found the Mercedes. The one taken from the motel in Waltham."

"Where?"

"Maryland," she said and flashed him a wolfish leer.

"Is there more?" He knew there would be.

"You're going to shit." She laughed and quickly added, "Sir."

He believed that he just might as she cut off a Trailways bus to zoom down the exit ramp nearest the airport.

6

"Those fifties were a good catch," Ted Brompton said.

"And a lucky break. Someone said their prayers last night," Bill said.

Bill was settled back in a tufted seat of buttery leather aboard the confiscated luxury jet. The upholstery was so inviting he wanted to sink into it and sleep all week. Starbucks made him jittery but not as awake as he needed to be. He bit the inside of his mouth hard enough to make his eyes water and concentrated on Brompton's words.

"Both bills trace back to an account the SEC was watching when Blanco first came on their radar. They recorded the serial numbers, sprayed them with UV paint and planted them in a stack of bills Blanco's wife withdrew from an account down in Boca."

"The deceased wife?"

"The honey you met up with in Boston. She's a player. Don't you worry; we have plenty to hold her on."

"Surprised the SEC went to all that trouble. Cloak and dagger stuff," Bill said.

Ted snorted. "It was the '90s, bro. Clinton was urging Treasury, IRS and Securities to climb up everyone's asses looking for revenue. He unleashed them."

"The ex-wife give up any more?"

"This invasion crew was after the big enchilada; a key of some kind to all of Blanco's offshore accounts. His rainy day fund. The way the former missus tells it, there was north of a billion five salted away," Ted said with a grin.

"A key?" Bill blinked.

"That's what Blanco told her. But no more than that. It's not an actual key; you can be damned sure of that. He also told her he had numbers for accounts that weren't his own. Other people's money. He could dip into them if he wanted. Whatever this key is, it's a double bonanza and a week in Hawaii for us, Treasury and the tax geeks. Throw in the SEC and FTA too. Careers will be made off of this."

"And she thinks this key was at the lake house?"

"She said he always liked that place best. He built it with the first million he stole. And he was paranoid about keeping too much overseas. Never knew when political winds could change."

"Then maybe our mystery man has this key?"

"That's the smart money."

"She give us a good description of our missing actor?" Bill said.

"Downloaded it on the way from Bangor." Ted handed over a tablet for Bill to look at.

A stern face looked back at Bill from the screen. It was a composite with all the qualities of a high-res photograph. The jawline and mouth matched what he could see under the hoodie in the Xtra Mart video. The eyes, usually lifeless in these recreations, had a predatory look about them. Well-set either side of a nose that had seen a few breaks. It was an intelligent face. Hard but intelligent.

"Facial recognition any help?" Bill said.

"Nada. It's iffy with these visualization programs. The ears and jaw only need to be a little off and we're eye-deeing Liam Neeson. But we may not need it."

"Yeah?"

"Our man got tangled in something in Maryland that the Baltimore PD and VSP are still sorting out."

"VSP?"

"Virginia State Police. We're close behind a possible last known location for this guy. He's ours. He just doesn't know it yet," Ted said with a lupine leer that was a mirror of the grin Agent Mandy had shared with Bill earlier.

Bill wasn't so sure. There was something about that face. Even in the compilation photo he sensed something feral, primal. There was too much about this guy they didn't know.

He kept his thoughts to himself and sank gratefully into the warm depths of the opulent chair and closed his eyes while Ted took a call from DC.

Gunny Leffertz said:
"Luck is no lady. Luck is a bitch. With you one second and gone the next."

7

Merry rested against him as he drove, her breathing soft. He hated to wake her but they were two exits from Roanoke.

Levon Cade drove with eyes shifting to the rear view and to the shoulders of the highway. The wipers slapped at the freezing rain marching in sheets out of the gray dawn light. He watched for the swirling lights of state troopers ahead and behind. By now, someone back in New Market would have found the body of the big man where he'd left it in the entryway of the flower shop. They'd find out who the dead man was. That would lead them to the GMC Sierra that Levon was now piloting south on 81.

He could feel the ring tightening around him. That sense of weight about to fall. He knew to trust that feeling.

The run down from Maine was a long one. It was only a matter of time before the police turned to the feds. And the feds would be putting the pieces together. They'd have an idea of what had happened up at Bellevue. They'd pick up the trail. They'd start stringing together events that would lead them south. He had hours. Maybe less.

Levon weighed speed against caution. He could stay to the highway and build distance between himself and the bodies he'd left behind. Or he could go to ground and wait out the hunt. Going to ground made more sense. If the FBI or multiple agencies were after him it wouldn't be a linear pursuit. They'd get ahead of him.

Simply running was not a solution. That required luck. And he knew he was way past luck. Fresh out of good fortune.

It would be pure D foolishness to underestimate the effort the government would make to find him. Through the fabric of his shirt, Levon's hand touched the lozenge shape that hung around his neck on a silver chain. The flash drive he'd taken from the thieves in Bellevue. It was what they'd gone to Maine to find. They killed for it. And at his hands, they died for it.

Whatever secrets the flash drive held were worth a global hunt by a crew of professionals. And if it was valuable to the thieves then it was valuable to the government. The little drive contained data that might lead to a Solomon's mine of untaxed millions hidden in banks around the world.

Levon had also taken a half million in cash and several millions in cut diamonds from the open vault. The feds wouldn't care about that. They wanted the little plastic stick swinging against his chest. If they got that, and got him, he'd do life on a list of federal charges. A half dozen or more homicides, a kidnapping or two, grand theft, at least three counts of auto theft, assault and whatever else they could tie him to depending on how much of the past two days they figured out. In addition, they could make a case that he was part of the robbery crew and make him an accomplice to all their prior offenses. They were dead. The justice meant for them would fall on him.

He needed to lose the Sierra and find other transport for them. He needed to get off the highway. And there was one more contingency that he didn't want to think about.

Levon's hand dropped to Merry's shoulder to steady her against him on the bench seat as he pulled off the first exit for Roanoke.

* * *

They left the Sierra on a municipal lot where it wouldn't be noticed. The rain had stopped. The light traffic on the street swished through the slush. Hand in hand, Levon and Merry walked a few blocks to a Hardee's that was open early for breakfast. The place gleamed jewel-like in the muted morning light.

There were kids Merry's age and older in the booths and at the counter. They had book bags and some wore school blazers. Levon took a seat and sent her to the counter to get their order. There would be cameras over the registers. An eleven-year-old girl wouldn't be noticed in the crowd of schoolkids.

Levon rested his boots against the gym bag and overnight bag that contained all he owned. Merry's backpack sat on the bench opposite him. Cartoon characters he didn't recognize capered across the fabric.

Merry came back with a tray loaded with egg and bacon sandwiches, hash brown patties, orange juice and a black coffee. He sipped coffee and watched her eat. There were dark circles under her eyes that he knew weren't from lack of sleep. The sight of her drawn face under strands of rain-drenched hair confirmed the way ahead for both of them.

They hiked down to the main street. No one would take a second look at a girl with a backpack. All the kids on the way to school had book bags. A grown man with a pair of bags would look like he was heading for the bus terminal a few blocks away. Levon found what he was looking for on a strip of stores set back from the street by a small parking lot.

Skyline Cell sold and repaired cell phones and personal devices. They carried satellite phones and prepaid cards for airtime. While Merry played on a display game device, Levon picked out phones and cards. The counter guy woke from a sleepy daze when Levon placed bills on the counter.

"How about a free ball cap?" the counter guy said, pulling down an adjustable cap with the Tracfone logo embroidered in gold against a black panel above the bill.

"No thanks," Levon said.

"It's free. They're gimmes from the company," the guy said and held the cap above the plastic bag he held open on the counter.

Levon shrugged. "Sure. Thanks."

A block away, Levon removed his sodden cap and stuffed it in a trash bin. He fitted the new cap to his head.

* * *

Merry went into a Rexall with a list from her father. She told the nosy counter woman that her mom and baby brother were homesick and had no one else to pick up the stuff they needed. If the woman wondered why her mother needed bandage strips, packing tape, and three books of postage stamps, she kept it to herself. Merry eyed herself in the HD surveillance image displayed on the monitor above the checkout.

At the post office, Levon filled out a packing label addressed to Gunny Leffertz in Mississippi. He affixed the label to the box containing one of the new satellite phones and then sealed the box all around with the packing tape before placing rows of enough postage stamps to send the package priority. Before all of that he recorded the sat phone's number on the back of a blank customs slip.

Since it was over thirteen ounces Merry took the package into the post office counter. A bored guy with a beard and a mustard stain on his USPS smock postmarked it and plastered Priority Mail stamps on every face of the box before tossing it in a bin with other parcels. If he noted that there was no return address marked on the box he didn't say anything.

"Thank you," Merry said and skipped through the door to the lobby. A buzzer sounded when the door swung open.

"Uh huh," said the bearded guy.

* * *

Levon and Merry sat on a bench under the shelter of a bus stop. Traffic had picked up as the morning moved on. From their vantage point, Levon could watch the parking lot of a community hospital. Merry dozed, her head down on the backpack in her lap.

A five-year-old Buick Lacrosse pulled onto the lot off the street. It made its way to spaces marked

Emergency Staff only. A slender young woman in royal blue scrubs under a down coat exited the car. She pulled the strap of a gear bag over her shoulder and walked to the entrance under the emergency awning.

Levon touched his daughter's shoulder to wake her. He asked, "What do you do if anything happens?"

"Walk away," she mumbled without raising her head.

"Good girl," he said and lifted the gym bag from the pavement and crossed the street to the hospital lot.

In under sixty seconds he was inside the Lacrosse. Its alarm squawked twice before he cut it off. Car alarms were part of the urban soundtrack. No one paid attention to them. He started the car, which smelled of recent marijuana use, and pulled off the lot. An emergency room nurse would be pulling at least a twelve-hour shift. That was enough lead time to get where he needed to be.

Merry, who had been watching, rose from the bus stop bench to meet him on the lot of a tire store. She carried the overnight in addition to her Adventure Time backpack. They were out of the city and rolling west on a county road.

"Is that mail on the dash?" Levon asked her.

"Yeah. Deborah Ianelli. She lives in Vinton," Merry read from the envelope of a gas company bill.

"We'll send her some cash for the use of the car," he said.

"Okay," she said and reclined her seat until her feet were dangling in the air.

The tires hissed on the wet road as they barreled under the bare limbs of trees arched above. They burst into watery sunlight when the woods gave way to rolling fields dappled with white left from earlier snow.

Merry spoke up when the Lacrosse plunged once more into the shelter of woods. "Daddy?"

"Yes, honey?"

"Why did you buy three of those phones?"

"Well, I was meaning to talk to you about that," he said and swallowed to clear his throat.

8

"I still don't see how this ties in," said Lieutenant Charles Rance of Virginia State Police CID.

Ted Brompton explained, "We're putting the pieces together ourselves." They sat at the counter of the My Way Hi-Way truck stop on 81.

Lieutenant Rance eyed the agent seated by Brompton. The man looked as if he slept in his clothes and was possibly hungover, face gray, hair lank and shoulders bowed where he bent over a plate of scrambled eggs and peppers smothered in hot sauce.

Bill Marquez listened to the exchange. He wolfed his scrambled, washing it down with pulls from a bottomless cup of black coffee. Long stake-outs had taught him something the academy didn't; if you can't get sleep, get calories.

Bill studied Rance once the big statie turned away. Guy was ex-military for sure. Skin dark as the coffee Bill was slamming down. Gray creeping in on the short-back-and-sides-cut hair, otherwise it was impossible to nail down the guy's age. Desert Storm vet maybe. The statie wore his tailored blue suit like a uniform; knife-edge creases, dazzling white shirt and conservative pale blue tie with a little pair of gold handcuffs pinning it in place. Bill felt like an unmade bed around a guy like this.

"So, a home invasion homicide in Maine two days ago ties into a homicide here in New Market last night?" Rance said, trying to keep up with Agent Brompton's timeline.

"That's the working theory. Can you share what you have?" Brompton smiled professionally.

Rance flipped open a notepad and read:

"Calvin Thomas Shepherd is the deceased. Multiple gunshots. Time of death sometime after midnight last night. He has a record but no convictions in Maryland and New Jersey. Assault mostly. Whoever shot him either used a revolver or picked up their brass. They worked close, too. CSI said there were powder burns on Shepherd's clothes."

Ted said, "He's tied in with a crew in Baltimore. We found three of them dead in a bar in Towson. Killed sometime yesterday afternoon."

"Dawson," Bill said around a mouthful of eggs and peppers.

"Right. How did Shepherd get here? You find a car?" Ted said.

"He had no keys on him. Maybe someone drove him here and killed him," the lieutenant said, flipping his pad closed.

"Or killed him and took his ride." Bill pushed the empty plate from him and jabbed a finger down at his empty mug for a wandering waitress to see.

"Did Baltimore give us a list of cars in Shepherd's name?" Ted said, turning his stool to Bill.

Bill touched his smartphone, scrolling until he found what he wanted. He picked the phone up and squinted, eyelids still gritty.

"A GMC Sierra. Forest Green. This year's model. Maryland plate. GXR-977."

"Then that's what he's driving," Ted said to the statie.

"That's what who is driving?" Rance said.

"That's what we'd like to know," Bill watched with greedy eyes as the waitress loaded up his mug.

The lieutenant called his superiors who put a BOLO out for the Sierra. As they walked out to their cars, he promised the two FBI agents to send along all the initial reports on Shepherd. He didn't expect any revelations.

Ted shrugged. "Rained like hell last night."

The agents thanked him and picked their way between puddles to the bureau car they'd gotten from the Baltimore office.

> Gunny Leffertz said:
> *"Move away from your attacker. Distance is your friend. Only break up your unit when pursuit is close."*

9

Merry slept most of the drive and when awake spoke only when spoken to. She was angry and hurt over what he had to tell her, the hard decision he was forced to make.

"You wanted to visit Gunny and Joyce."

She turned to the window, voice breaking. "With you. But you won't be there."

"I don't want it to be this way, honey."

"Then keep driving. Just drive till we both get there."

"I can't. I explained why I can't."

"I don't want to go alone."

"And I don't like the idea either. This is the best way. The only way. I'm all out of options. You have to be brave."

She wouldn't answer him. They rode in silence.

It was after midnight when Levon pulled into the lot of the America's Best Value Inn in Murphysboro, Illinois. The drive from Virginia had taken fourteen hours. Two hours added to the straight through drive because he stuck to county roads until they were well into Tennessee. He got them on Route 40 at Knoxville around three in the afternoon.

Levon checked himself into a single room using the story that his wife kicked him out of the house. His father-in-law, a mean son of a bitch, was over to the house. He didn't have time to get his wallet, he just got his ass the hell out of there. A buddy lent him a couple hundred.

"Whydn't you stay with your buddy?" the guy at the desk asked more out of idle curiosity and desire for conversation on a slow night.

"He's married to my wife's sister," Levon said, shit-eating grin in place.

The guy barked at that and slid the room card to him.

After checking for cameras Levon met Merry at a back exit. There were none and he let her in. They used the stairs to reach the room. Without a word she locked herself in the bathroom. He lay back on the bedcovers to close his eyes for a second. He could hear the shower running.

That was the last thing he heard before he awakened to the drag and boom of truck traffic out on the highway. Sunlight was streaming in through a gap in the drapes. Merry was asleep in an armchair pulled up close in front of the TV, curled in a ball under a quilt. A smiling man and woman on the TV were making something in a dream kitchen, clean white aprons worn over immaculate clothes. The volume was reduced to a sibilant mutter.

He took a long shower, thought about shaving and decided that it should wait.

When he came out of the bathroom, Merry had moved to the bed. She lay under the covers, facing the window, her back to him.

Levon dressed and went to see about getting them breakfast.

* * *

He walked to an IHOP down the road from the hotel. The Lacrosse was backed into a space at the rear of the lot behind the America's Best. It wouldn't draw attention to itself. Cheaters parked that way to hide their plates.

Merry was as he left her when he got back with two plastic bags of take-out waffles in clamshell containers. The smell was enough to lure her out from under the covers. She ate in silence, digging into a stack of strawberry shortcake waffles. She nodded when he held up maple syrup packets.

She wasn't angry, wasn't sullen. When she did look at him it was with an expression of heartbreaking sadness. He knew she was hurting at the idea of them separating. He couldn't help but read into it a resentment about all that he'd put her through since they left Huntsville almost a year ago.

Levon knew his little girl would never hold that against him. Since her mother died, Merry accepted that life was capable of cruel surprise. A hard thing for an eleven-year-old to deal with, even harder for Levon to take on. A father was supposed to shield his child from trouble, not bring more on. And she had no idea of half of the trouble he invited into their lives when he'd agreed to go hunting for Jim Wiley's daughter. He was a wanted man. The only grandparents Merry knew were dead. They lived on the road, changing names and homes.

His decision was a hard one to make. But it was

best for her and that's all that mattered.

Even though these next few days would not be the happiest between them, they were still precious to him. Waiting in this hotel room, eating take-out and watching TV wasn't anyone's idea of quality time. But they were together and that would have to be enough for him and, hopefully, enough for Merry when she looked back on it.

For now, they were waiting out the days until Gunny got the package he'd mailed the day before.

After seventy-two near-straight hours of wakeful-ness, Bill felt like he was watching the landscape go by through the wrong end of a telescope. He wished he could be the next FBI agent shot in the line of duty just so he'd have permission to lie down.

"You look like shit," Ted said, eying him from behind wheel.

"I feel like shit," he replied, drooping against his shoulder strap.

"Lexington is coming up. I'm dropping you off for some rack time. There's nothing going on right now anyway."

Bill could only nod. Even that motion was a su-preme effort.

Ted dumped him off at a Day's Inn close to the highway.

Ted called from the car, "Take a shower. Get your clothes pressed. And get some sleep. I can give you six hours max."

Bill waved. He slumped toward the entrance, bag slung over his shoulder. The automatic doors hissed open and warm, welcoming canned air swept over him from within. He thought he heard angels singing but it was only Abba on the lobby PA system.

* * *

Showered and wrapped in a towel, Bill lay back atop the covers on his economy double bed and punched in the numbers to reach Nancy Valdez at Treasury. He wasn't sure why he was calling her. All he knew was that, beat as he was, he wouldn't be able to sleep without talking to her. She was his confessor and sleep was his communion. The nuns would approve of that analogy, he thought as he listened to the Brahms piano concerto that served as hold music for the T-men.

"They've brought me in on this Maine thing," Nancy told him once he reached her.

"Yeah?"

"Same as the bureau brought you in. My background on this. They're putting together a cross-agency task force. A hump from DHS is taking lead."

"What's Homeland's interest here?" Bill said.

"They found a pickup truck up at the Maine site registered to the Mitchell Roeder alias. An automatic rifle and lots of ammo were found concealed in it. That's all they need to claim domestic terrorism."

"Brompton's not going to be happy about that."

"Who's that?"

"Agent I'm working under. He thinks he's lead on this."

She said, "He's not lead as of an hour ago. The Blanco ex is talking a blue streak to save her ass. I don't have details but she swears that whatever the guys in this crew were looking for was in the Maine house. I have to bite my tongue to keep from saying 'told you so.'"

"What about Tex? Roeder? The guy on the run?" he said with a yawn.

"She says he wasn't with the crew. Just the right guy showing up at the wrong time. She followed him to Waltham and braced him. She thought, as Blanco's only surviving ex, she was entitled to a piece of whatever he got away with."

"She know his real name? Where he's heading?"

"She knew him as Mitch Roeder from Arkansas. That matches a—" He heard her tapping keys. "—a Mitchell Jennings Roeder, born in Jonesboro. Born in '85. Died in a car accident aged four. It's a professional identity appropriation. This guy either paid a lot or had help."

"But he is a southern boy."

"Well, according to the ex he is. Of course, she's Boston born. Anyone south of Philadelphia sounds like Reba McEntire to her. Guy could be from anywhere from Indiana to the Florida Keys. And the composite isn't much good."

"A bulletproof false ID," Bill said, "and he knows how to defeat facial recognition and elude a combined state, local and federal dragnet. And he brought down a crew of badasses all by himself. Think he's one of us? Or was one of us?"

"Does sound like he has skills, doesn't it?" Nancy said.

"Or former military."

"You sound tired." The cynical cool had melted from her voice.

"You have no idea," he said and watched the ceiling swimming in and out of focus.

"The world will still be here when you wake up."

"That's what I'm afraid of, Nancy."

"Good night, Bill."

He was already gone, the cell phone tumbling from his hand to the carpet.

11

It was flurrying snow when the taxi pulled up under the apron at the entrance of the America's Best. A big guy in work boots squeezed his way into the cramped confines of the minivan's rear seat. The driver eyeballed the guy in the rearview. He looked like he was dressed to go deer hunting. Or, with a heavy growth of beard on his jaw, maybe fresh back from a deer camp.

"Where to?" the driver said.

"You tell me . . . Phil," the big man said, leaning forward to read the driver's name off the ID plate on dash.

"What's the supposed to mean?" said the driver whose name was not Phil. That was his cousin who owned the hack and allowed a couple of family members to rack up hours behind the wheel, though that was not strictly legal. In truth, it was entirely illegal.

"I'm new in town. I don't know where to go." With an easy smile, the big man rested back on the seat.

"And I'm supposed to tell you?" not-Phil said,

studying his passenger in the reflection.

The big guy leaned forward, a fifty folded between his fingers. "Just a few helpful suggestions, you being a local."

"Help me out, son. Are you thirsty or are you lonely?" Not-Phil took the fifty and slipped it into the breast pocket of his shirt.

"Lonely."

"I know just the place," not-Phil, said and put the mini in gear to roll out toward the highway to enter the stream of golden lights flowing past in the winter gloom.

* * *

The place was a single home in what was once a blue-collar neighborhood in nearby Carbondale. The house glowed amber under twinkle lights left up long after Christmas. They gave off a dismal rather than festive effect. A four bedroom with a three-car carport on a half-acre lot enclosed by cyclone fencing. Two Dobermans trotted around the yard. The snow was mottled with their feces.

A train passed by in the dark close enough that Levon could hear the clank of the coupler heads as it slowed into a yard.

The driver handed over his business card.

"For the drive back," not-Phil said.

"Thanks." Levon let him keep the fifty for a twenty dollar fare.

A waist-high gate opened from the sidewalk onto a paved walkway lined either side with cyclone fencing creating a lane all the way to the front door. The two dogs loped beside him, heads held low, sniffing through the links. Not a sound out of either of them.

They were biters.

At the barred front door he pressed a doorbell. A voice spoke from an intercom. A man's voice. Gruff.

"What house are you looking for?"

"This one," Levon said and held up the cab driver's business card to the lens of the camera mounted above the door inside a mirrored plastic dome.

There was a buzz and a click and Levon turned the knob and entered.

The impression of a typical suburban home ended once he was inside. A cramped foyer with paneled walls and a single steel door mounted to the left. To his right was an opening that resembled a teller's booth in a bank. It was fronted by a pane of Lexan with a pay slot built in at the bottom. The once-clear plastic was yellowed by years of nicotine. An immensely fat man sat behind the pane in a brightly lit room no bigger than a closet. He wore suspenders over a shirt decorated with red roses. A half-eaten apple pie sat by him on a narrow counter. He stuck a fork in the crust. He inclined his head to look at Levon through glasses perched on the end of his nose.

"I don't know you."

The same razor-gargling voice Levon had heard over the intercom.

"I've never been here before," Levon said.

"Andy sent you?" That must have been not-Phil's real name.

"He drove me here. Just dropped me off."

"You're not a cop. I know all the cops," the fat man said without a trace of accusation in his tone.

"Me? A cop?" Levon acted as if the suggestion was both amusing and ludicrous.

"There's a menu on the wall. Prices are not negotiable." The fat man poked a sausage finger to his right.

Levon stepped closer to read a printed page enclosed in a plastic sheet that was tacked to the paneling. It listed, in graphic and unmistakable terms, the services offered and the prices demanded. Costs went all the way to five hundred dollars. A notice in the bottom in yellow highlight stated that "each additional party to any of the above services requires an additional charge equal to the price of the selected service."

"You want a white girl? A black one? We have an Asian girl but you'll have to wait for her," the fat man announced through the slot.

Levon stepped back to the Lexan and stood to one side of the waist-high cash slot.

"I was looking for something not on the menu," Levon said.

The fat man glanced away from his pie, his eyes narrowed. His mouth turned down in a wet frown.

"I don't want any trouble and I'm not going to have any."

"Slow down. It's not like whatever you're thinking it is," Levon said, smiling easy, hands held up before him.

"Then what is it?"

"I need papers. Eye-dee. They don't have to be the best. Just enough to get me where I'm going," Levon said.

"Now's when I ask you if you're cop. Are you a cop?"

"Thought you knew all the cops."

"All the cops in the county. Not all the cops in

the state."

"I'm not a cop. State, federal or otherwise. I'm just a guy who needs to be someone else for a while. And I need it quick."

"Quick is expensive," the fat man said, eyeing Levon's workman clothes.

Levon counted out five hundred in fifties and twenties and placed them on the smooth sill of the cash slot. The fat man grasped them, all interest in the pie forgotten. He tugged on the bills but Levon maintained his grip.

"Driver's license, any state. And something with a matching address. Utility bill or like that. And an insurance company card," Levon said, meeting the other man's piggy eyes through the hazed pane.

"Bring twice this much back tomorrow."

Levon released his grip. The fat man plucked the bills away.

"What time?"

"We open at one in the afternoon. I should have what you need by then."

Levon nodded.

"What about a picture?" the fat man said.

Levon placed a flat square of plastic the size of a postage stamp on the counter and slid it through the slot. It was the photo cut from his Mitch Roeder driver's license.

"This do?"

"Sure. You staying awhile? Your money's good here," the fat man said, nodded toward the menu.

"Maybe another time. Buzz me out," Levon said and stepped out into the cold.

12

Bill Marquez was rested and restless. Two days of doubling back, re-reading notes, re-questioning sources, left him sour. He was ready to punch a hole in a wall.

Mitch Roeder's, AKA Tex, trail died in Roanoke.

They found the GMC truck that belonged to Calvin Shepherd on a city lot. There was a report from Roanoke PD of a stolen Buick taken off a hospital lot. Could be their man. If it was he had a twelve-hour head start and could be in any one of seven states by now.

Ted Brompton got Bill his own car and sent him back upstream to talk to witnesses. The night counter guy at the Dogwood in New Market critiqued the composite image. He'd gotten a good look at the guy. Described, as best he could, the little girl, too. Witness descriptions of kids weren't worth shit generally. Men really never looked at kids unless they were pervs. Women were better at descriptions of children; they noticed things like eye color and clothing.

The counter guy remembered that Roeder went outside. Pointed to the front door of the Dogwood, the street sunny now with afternoon light.

"But it was pissing rain that night. Said he wanted a smoke. He came back inside after a little bit, paid for the check with a twenty and took the little girl out with him."

That would have been when Shepherd was killed only a few doors away.

"Anyone else here that night?" Bill asked.

"Someone was in one of the other booths. A local, I think. A regular. Give me a second and I'll remember," the counter guy said, nodding to an empty booth behind Bill.

"Anyone else you do remember?"

"Two deputies. Howard Chase and Barry Tillotson. But they had their backs to the guy the whole time. We were talking basketball," the counter guy said.

"I'll talk to them anyway. You never know." Bill went for his wallet to pay for the tuna sandwich and Coke he ordered. The counter guy waved him off.

"Take it off my taxes," he joked.

Bill faked a chuckle and turned to leave.

"Hey, can we start using the ladies room again?" the guy said, gesturing to the door at the back of the place. There was yellow crime scene tape across the opening of a room marked GALS.

Bill shrugged. "Sure. We got all we can out of there."

Bill drove over to the sheriff's annex and caught the two deputies clocking in for the four to midnight. Neither of them had seen a damned thing. Had their backs to the perp the whole time. One of them actually used the word "perp."

Everyone watches too goddamn much television, Bill thought as he backed the bureau Chevy out from the row of black and tan county cars.

He pulled onto 81 and drove north toward DC. Tex's possible route down from New Haven was starting to come together and they had gathered footage from bridges, toll booths and red light cameras. More videos were trickling in from gas stations, discount stores and fast food drive-thrus. There was a team reviewing video. A model was being built backtracking Tex and his daughter all the way back to Lake Whatsis in Maine.

Ted wanted him to wrangle the team and apply pressure for results. It was bureaucratic gravity in effect. DHS was applying pressure to Ted to bring them some good news. Ted was raining shit down on every agent below him.

The current administration was positively sex-mad for homegrown terrorists of the non-Islamic variety. They were always making a case for the danger of militias and white supremacy groups. Anyone in fed law enforcement knew this was boogeyman stuff. The only militias Bill had ever seen were weekend warriors out playing Rambo in the woods. Tubby guys who got bored reenacting Civil War battles and wanted to play with semi-automatic rifles instead of muskets.

And the racist groups were even sadder. They mostly spent their time in court fighting for permits to join parades or set up booths at state fairs. When they weren't doing that they were making videos for their web sites. It was Bill's opinion that they should run those videos during the Super Bowl and let the whole country see what a bunch of pathetic assholes these master race dickheads were.

To get the task force that the bureau and Treasury wanted, Ted let the political animals at Homeland think the guy they were chasing was the next Timothy McVeigh. That allowed them to tap the IRS and the NSA for Intel. Hell, the IRS had four times the agents that the G-men and T-men had.

It was all bullshit anyway. Whoever Tex was, he was a loner. Except for the little girl, of course. But Bill had a gut feeling this guy was more dangerous than a whole compound of survivalist crazies.

When Nancy Valdez called, he shared this with her over the car phone.

"Look at the way he's played us. Slipped the knot like a pro. Add that to the shit pile of corpses he left in Maine and whatever he got himself into with that Baltimore crew," Bill told her as he drove north toward the beltway.

"He's trained and he's smart. And if the former Mrs. Blanco is right he has the keys to the national debt of Bolivia," Nancy said from the speaker on the dash.

"I don't hear office noise."

"I'm not in the office."

"Are you home?" he asked.

"Next you're going to ask me what I'm wearing." He could hear her smile when she said it.

"I'm guessing a Glock."

"Fuck you. It's a Sig. I wouldn't touch a Glock with your dick."

"Whoa, lady! This is a government line you're on."

"So, where you heading next?"

"Just did my last interview. They called me back

to Quantico. Due diligence and background with the task force," Bill said.

"That's where they have me. I'm heading out the door right now," she said, her voice bright.

"I'll see you there then."

"See you."

Bill tabbed END CALL on the dash monitor. A car honked its horn and flashed high beams as he passed it on the right. He looked at the display. He was doing ninety-two in a sixty zone.

13

"You're going to make me fat, woman," Gunny said, pushing himself away from the table.

"Don't blame that on me, old man," Joyce said, standing to clear the dinner plates away. Dinner was pan fried perch with her signature rice pilaf.

"Let me help with that." He lifted his own plate from the table.

"Put that down," she scolded, playfully slapping the back of his hand. "You've broken enough of my dishes."

"Should buy plastic ware like I been telling you."

"Both of us have spent enough years eating off plastic. My table will have real china and real silver," she said, and elbowed him from the table.

"You're treating me like a helpless old blind man again," he said, stepping back as she brushed by him.

"I'm treating you like a clumsy old blind man. If you want to help you can dry. But I'll put them away."

"You want the news on?"

"I'm sick and tired of the news. Put on some music

or something." She placed the dishes in one sink and the silver in another and turned on the water.

Gunny made his way into the great room, piloting down three steps and between furniture with practiced ease, to the Bose. He snapped it on to let the liquid tones of Buddy Guy's six-string fill the cabin. He was returning to the kitchen to help with the drying when a two-tone beep sounded under the opening bars of "Sweet Little Angel."

"What the hell is that?" he said. He heard dishes splashing into soapy water. Joyce's footfalls approached.

"It's that satellite phone that came today," she said, walking past him, a hand brushing his arm.

Joyce picked the phone off the charger.

He heard her greet the caller then listen in silence for a beat or two before telling the caller that Gunny was with her.

"Levon," she said, and took Gunny's offered hand and placed the phone in his palm.

"Talk to me, Slick," Gunny said.

* * *

"You don't have to do this," he told her.

"You're going to drive to Memphis? I'd pay to see that, Gunny," Joyce said.

They were out on the gravel drive. The night was cold under a sky sprayed with stars against velvet black. The cabin was a half day's ride from anywhere so the nights were true dark. Gunny had no need of light and Joyce was used to using only a minimum of illumination. She wasn't sure why but it made her feel closer to him.

Joyce took the overnight bag from Gunny's hand

and placed it in the back seat of their Dodge Ram's crew cab.

"When I get back I'll drive Levon's truck way up the deer road and leave it there," Joyce said. The truck was an Avalanche with Alabama plates left here by Levon Cade over a year ago. He'd received Joyce's tired old Range Rover in trade.

"I still wish you'd let me go with you," Gunny said, running his hand down her arm.

"You think I can't handle a drive to Memphis and back?"

"It's not that."

"You get car sick anyway."

"Didn't used to. Started driving when I was fourteen. My daddy's tractor, my uncle's Dodge truck."

"And you walked five miles to school, uphill both ways. Next you'll be telling me war stories. Why don't you just say you'll miss me?" She pulled him close.

"It's just that it's a lot to ask, is all," he said, his arms about her, crushing her to him. His rock, his anchor.

"For you?"

"For me. For Levon. That boy's in trouble or he'd never ask."

"He means a lot to you so he means a lot to me. That's all I need to know. There's oatmeal for breakfast already made in the fridge so you don't make a mess of my kitchen. And use the micro to warm it. You burn down my kitchen and it's your ass, old man."

"Sir, yes, sir!" he said, breaking the embrace and taking a step back.

"And don't you ever forget I outranked you." She

smiled and leaned forward to kiss him on the cheek before getting behind the wheel.

"Thank you, Joyce," he said, closing the rear door for her.

"I'll be back by lunch tomorrow. Mind your toes," she said and pulled away.

He stood listening to the crunch of the tires on gravel until the sound faded away to be covered by the swish of tree branches swaying on the night breeze.

14

The driver's license was bargain basement. It was the best he was going to do for a thousand bucks in a small town. The watermarks were blurry at the edges and the embedded hologram of the state emblem was crooked. The laminate was too shiny. He scuffed it on the edge of a table, both sides, until the sheen was gone.

He was Oscar Bruckman of Tulsa. The age was close enough as were his height and eye color. Oscar was a redhead but lots of guys dyed their hair these days. It was one-time use. No one was going to be looking that close.

The man at the Amtrak ticket window needed a shave. He barely glanced at the driver's license resting in the tray. He seemed more interested in the Band-Aids that Levon wore on the lobes of his ears.

"The wife got me gold studs for Christmas. Believe that?" Levon said with a crooked smile.

"Ah," the Amtrak man said.

"They got infected as hell. A doctor had to cut them out." Levon winced.

"You wife went someplace cheap," the Amtrak man said with a sympathetic wince.

"Mall kiosk. But she was so happy, you know?"

"The things we do for love." The man shrugged and bent to retrieve the printed ticket from a machine below the counter.

"Oh yeah."

"Your little girl is traveling alone?" The man glanced over Levon's shoulder to where Merry sat solemn on a long wooden bench in the waiting area. Her chin rested on the backpack resting on her knees.

"Going down to visit her grandparents in Texas. She'll be there tomorrow morning, right?"

"Most days. You're lucky we had a sleeping compartment free."

"I feel better if she has a sleeper. She has a door she can lock, you know?"

"You can go down to the platform with her and meet the train. Talk to the attendant on her car. They'll look after her." The guy slid the ticket envelope through the tray slot.

"Thanks for your help." Levon slipped the ticket envelope into his coat pocket.

He took Merry into a small vending area off the lobby. It was lined with soda and candy machines. They were alone there. He took the silver chain from around his neck and draped it around Merry's. He tucked the flash drive out of sight beneath her sweater.

"What do you do with this?" he said.

"Keep it hidden," she said. Her eyes were still red from crying.

"And when you see Gunny?"

"Give it to him and tell him you want him to hide it."

"And?"

"And not tell me or anyone else where he hides it."

"Good girl."

They walked together down to the platform. Dawn was an hour or more away. A wind blew snow across the open platform in gusts of powder that glowed silver under the lights.

He crouched to secure a name tag to the strap of her backpack and another to a button loop on the collar of her coat. The name and address were false.

"I'm not a baby," she said, glaring with a baleful expression at the name tag hanging from her collar.

"It's just to keep you and your bag together, okay?"

She sat on a bench. He stood watching the empty tracks for the train's arrival. It was a whistle stop station and they were alone on the platform except for a couple of workers in reflective vests. They were joking and laughing as they brushed away a dusting of snow with push brooms.

The train thundered into the station to a stop. A few people exited the coach cars. Levon walked Merry forward to the sleepers and met the uniformed attendant for her car.

Her name was Daneeta, a heavy-set black woman who had a big smile for Merry. She took Merry's backpack and read the name tag.

"You're with us all the way to San Antonio, changing in New Orleans, Megan?"

Merry nodded.

"Megan, you're a lucky girl. We'll be serving breakfast soon and it's included with your ticket."

"I'm not really hungry," Merry said, eyes lowered.

"I thought she could just stay in her cabin," Levon said.

"Don't you worry, Dad. I'll look after Megan. And we have a one-hour layover in New Orleans. I'll stay with her until she gets on her next train. That okay?"

Levon nodded, eyes on Merry turned away from him.

"You're in 'D,' sweetheart. Down on your left," Daneeta said and helped Merry up into the car.

Levon picked up the yellow steel step stool and held it up to the attendant. There was a pair of hundred dollar bills under his thumb.

"You sure, sir?" Daneeta asked.

At her response to the generous tip Levon felt a knot in the pit of his stomach unravel a turn or two.

"That's my little girl. Don't let her fill up on waffles, okay?" Levon said, smiling easy.

"Yes, sir." Daneeta slid the door into place.

The train rumbled and jerked. Levon walked forward to watch it leave the station. He looked to the windows of the sleeper, looking for Merry. As the train pulled away he saw her in the corner of one of the windows. She met his eyes and flexed her fingers for a wave that offered a treaty between them.

He was making her grow up too fast, making her accept the kind of challenges he wished he could have protected her from. The train rolled on into the dark until it was just a triangle of lights vanishing around a turn under a pewter sky.

15

Levon took the overnight and gym bag out of a locker. He entered a cab outside the Carbondale station. He had to wake the driver. The cab dropped him off at a professional park he'd found in the phone book the night before. It was a collection of stand-alone buildings housing insurance broker offices, a pediatrician, four dentists, a weight loss center and a podiatrist. The parking spaces on the tree-dotted lot were empty at this hour.

He took a window booth at a Denny's that sat road front on the same lot as the pro park. From his seat he could see cars pulling off the four-lane into the park. He ate breakfast and nursed a coffee. The sky reddened and the dark turned to blobs then streaks of shadows.

A few cars entered the lot, their headlights making a nimbus glow then dying when the drivers found parking spaces. He waited until a dozen cars had arrived before paying his check and cutting from the Denny's through a line of low hedges onto the pro-park lot.

He picked out a Chrysler 200 parked across from a cosmetic dentistry office. The license plate read SMLE. He touched the hood. Still warm. The owner would be here until at least lunchtime, or more than likely all day. More than enough time. A thin band of tensile steel between the window and door frame and the lock post popped up. Inside the still-warm car, he defeated the alarm and hot-wired the ignition.

Piloting through a snarl of overpasses, Levon took a ramp for 55 and headed northwest for the two-hour drive to St. Louis.

* * *

The sky was turning pink over gray winter fields. Merry watched fence posts whip by through the window by her table. She sat in the dining car.

The waiter's name was Leonard and he was very funny. "How would you like your eggs, miss? Scrambled? Over easy? Omelet?" He rocked with movement of the train, pencil poised over his pad.

"Scrambled is fine," she said.

"Chicken, duck or ostrich?" Leonard said with a tilt of his head, eyes grave.

"What?" she said, looking up at him. Leonard was an older man with a shaved head and trim white mustache. He wasn't smiling.

"We have penguin eggs, too. But not many people want them. They're always cold," Leonard said with a shrug.

Merry held a hand over her mouth to stifle a giggle.

"That's what I like to see in the morning," Leonard said and beamed at her. "I'll bring you some fresh-squeezed orange juice to start."

He walked back toward the noisy kitchen area with a sailor's gait. The car swayed side-to-side.

The tables in the dining car were empty but for an elderly couple seated behind her. Daneeta, the attendant, told her that the car would be full once the sun was up.

"This way you get to eat your breakfast in peace, sweetheart," Daneeta had said before heading back to the sleeping cars.

The sun was clearing the horizon. The train passed through woods; Merry could see the sun flashing between the boles of trees. The table bumped under her elbow. In the reflection of the dark glass, she saw someone had taken a seat across from her.

"Hi, what's your name?" the man said. He smiled, thick cheeks rising to turn his eyes to slits behind thick glasses. There was sweat on his forehead even though the car was chilled with morning cold.

Merry looked back out the window, pretending interest in the view.

"My name is Axel." The man reached a hand across the table. Her hands remained on the table, holding her juice glass steady. He took the hand back.

"It's lonely traveling alone. I'm by myself, too. No one to share the adventure with."

She wished he would go away. From the corner of her eye, she saw him pick up a menu card.

"I think I'll have coffee. Amtrak serves the best coffee. A lot of people don't know that. You probably don't drink coffee. Too young, huh?"

His voice changed. It was low now, meant only for her. The sound of a smile was gone from it.

"We could be friends, couldn't we? Someone to talk to? It's all right. I take the train all the time. I like meeting new people. You don't need to be so shy."

She shut her eyes, willing him to go away.

"It's okay to talk. Be friendly. A stranger's just a friend you haven't met. You ever hear that before?"

Merry opened her eyes. A swimming white shape appeared in the glass against the leaden dawn light.

"There are plenty of other seats, sir," Leonard said. He set down plates in front of Merry. Leonard was smiling. But it wasn't a real smile. His eyes locked on the man, lids narrow.

"I'm comfortable here. You can bring some coffee," the man said, his smile fixed.

"I think you'd be more comfortable at another table," Leonard said, hands braced on the edges of the table.

"I'm fine here."

"Let's ask the lady then. Would you like to have your breakfast alone, miss?" Leonard said, his smile gone.

Merry nodded.

"That's it then. I'll bring your coffee to your new table." Leonard placed a hand under the man's arm as though to help him from his seat.

The man rose with a last glance at Merry before allowing himself to be ushered to a table closer to the kitchen.

Merry watched from under her brows as she ate her eggs and toast. Keeping an eye on the man who called himself Axel, careful not to let him catch her. He was still eating his breakfast when she stood to return to the sleeping car.

She slipped a butter knife up her sleeve before sliding away from the table.

16

The Buick LaCrosse was practically family to Deborah Ianelli. When she found the car missing from the emergency staff lot, her first call was to GloboTrac, the firm that provided GPS monitoring for her car. Her second call was to the Roanoke police.

She was tired after a twelve-hour shift in the ER. She stayed on the lot to talk to the cops who responded to her call. She gave them her license and registration. One cop asked questions while another entered the car onto a stolen vehicle list on the computer in the cop car. They assured her that the car was as good as found. "Probably some kids joyriding."

Another nurse gave her a ride home to her one bedroom in Vinton. Debbie wanted nothing more than a hot shower and bed. But she sat at the counter in the kitchenette and stayed on the phone with GloboTrac, working her way through an information tree until she reached an actual human being. Then she moved up the chain until she had someone who called himself "Larry" in a thick Mumbai accent.

"Where's my car, Larry?" she said when he took a breath from his scripted greeting.

"It is not showing up on our system," Larry said with sorrow.

"I pay you every month for this service. You're telling me it doesn't work? Where's my car?"

"It is no longer in the coverage area. Or possibly your transmitter is malfunctioning." Again he was reading. Probably from a troubleshooter screen.

"This is GloboTrac, right? Global tracking. Global. That means the whole world."

"Yes?"

"So how can my car be out of the coverage area? Is my car on the Moon?"

"No?"

"Where's my car, Larry?"

Two days later her Buick Lacrosse was found at the ass-end of a Walmart lot in Carbondale, Illinois and reported back to the VSP auto theft division. The car was on a watch list for vehicles recently stolen in the state. The recovery was passed on from state CID to the FBI who told Carbondale PD to keep their greasy hands off the Buick until crime scene techs arrived.

Bill Marquez was dispatched to Carbondale on follow-up. No luxury jet this time. Just a lonely drive in a bureau car.

From the dash speaker Nancy Valdez said, "Admit it, you called me because you're bored."

"It's business," he said. The four-lane stretched empty before him but for the red lights of a truck in the right lane far ahead.

"Nothing on the radio? You're bored."

"Maybe it's because I miss you."

"It was only dinner, Agent Marquez," she said with a dry chuckle.

"I enjoyed it. I want to see you again when I get back," he said.

"But I pick the place this time. Chain restaurant pasta ne'er won fair lady."

"I promise. Someplace with tablecloths and a wine list."

"So, is there really any business here? You called on a bureau number. Make it good, agent."

"I'm checking on a car stolen in Roanoke. Wound up in Illinois. Feels right. Sounds like a getaway to me," he said.

"Think he reached his destination?" she said.

"This guy's no thug. If he was at the end of his run we'd never have found the stolen ride. How in the loop are you on this?"

"Treasury is working the currency angle. I'm lead on that. Another suspect bill showed up in Lexington. Trail goes dead after that."

"As lead you must be getting general updates. You have a better seat than me. I'm just running errands here. A rat in the maze."

"The updates bring no joy, Bill. They're sorting through video surveillance along his probable route. Nothing's come up on facial recognition but there's like a million hours of video to go through. Fingerprint and DNA evidence up in Maine at the Waltham motel came up nada."

"No fingerprints? Nothing? The guy was living in the house for months with the little girl."

"There's plenty of evidence. Only no matches. The guy's not in the system."

"Bullshit. Homeland is sending out tweets on their

fuck-ups now? That doesn't sound like something they'd include on a cross-agency update," he said.

"I know a guy who knows a guy at DHS."

"Does he pick better restaurants?"

"Silly. Look, I have other calls. Ring me when you get where you're going." Nancy broke the connection. Bill touched the screen on the dash to end the call.

He was telling her the truth. This Buick was taken by the guy they were all looking for. There was no way to explain how he knew. It was a feeling. And he'd learned to trust those feelings.

Gunny Leffertz said:
"If you know the enemy can see you then make damn sure they see what you want them to see."

17

He bought a pack of razors at a Target and shaved the beard off in the men's room. Then a stop at a Home Depot in Brentwood before driving to Lambert-St. Louis International. At Delta arrivals he pulled up to the curb and left the Chrysler there, motor running.

Levon found lockers where he secured the gym bag. He walked through to departures and tried to buy round trip tickets to Phoenix at the Southwest counter on a flight leaving in the next three hours. He wanted to use cash which caused the girl at the counter to take a closer than usual look at his phony license. She glanced toward a supervisor who stepped to the counter to find Levon counting out hundreds on the counter.

"Mister ... Bruckman?" the super said, glancing at the wrong license with a jaundiced gaze. The super was a middle-aged woman with the air of someone who's seen it all and heard every excuse.

"You don't have a credit card?" she said, studying him hard. There were at least three cameras trained on the counter. Three that he could see, anyway.

"I kind of had to leave the house in a hurry this morning," Levon said with a conspiratorial squint.

"Without your wallet?"

"Marie and me, that's my wife, had a little blow-up over some charges on the cards. I gave them up to her, proving a point, you know? I want to get the hell out of here before she hooks up with the Visa and finds out what some of those charges were for." He grinned, eyes darting away.

"We can't take cash payment for flights leaving today. That's Southwest policy." The super's tone went from skeptical to icy.

"Okay, okay. Can I book for tomorrow? I can stay at a hotel, I guess."

"Do you have any other form of identification, Mr. Bruckman?" she said.

"Sure. Sure," Levon said, patting his coat pockets until he came up with a folded electric bill made out to Oscar L. Bruckman.

The bill was from IGS Energy at an Illinois address. The super's eyes moved to the Oklahoma driver's license. She handed both back and nodded to the counter girl who took Levon's cash payment for an afternoon flight to Phoenix the following day. He received a receipt and was told to report to this same counter for a boarding pass at least two hours before take-off.

Levon walked the length of the arrivals area passing counters for a half dozen airlines. Through the window wall at the front of Delta he could see the Chrysler being secured to the hook of a tow truck. He turned back to the lockers to retrieve the gym bag then on to exit through the departures lounge. An airport bus took him to long range parking.

He chose a clean Chevy Tahoe parked less than an hour before. He paid for parking using the ticket he found atop the dash. From there it was off the lot onto a surface road that took him to I-70 where he powered up a westbound ramp.

* * *

Merry woke to find the train was not moving. She wondered if that was what woke her up after the gentle pitching of the car caused her to doze off. She looked through the window. Trees grew close to the tracks. She heard a rapping on the door of her compartment.

She undid the latch and pulled the door aside creating an eight-inch gap.

It was the man from the dining car. Axel. He smiled, looking down at her through thick lenses. He was close enough for her to smell the cloying chemical scent of his aftershave. He leaned his head through the door, eyes sweeping the tiny compartment.

"I thought maybe you'd like to talk some more," he said, planting a foot in the compartment, forcing Merry to back away. The backs of her legs touched one of the two seats facing one another in the closet-sized space.

"I was asleep," she said.

"I see that. You have sleepers in your eyes," he said, looming closer, reaching out a hand for her face.

She jerked back, dropping back into the seat. He was fully within the compartment now, head bent to speak to her, shaking his head.

"I only wanted to clear your eyes," he said, stooping toward her as, with his other hand, he began to pull the steel door closed.

Reaching down between the seat cushion and the chair arm, Merry's fingers found the handle of the butter knife she'd taken from the dining car. Her fist tightened on the handle. It seemed like such a small and pitiful weapon now.

"There's been a delay. I don't get off in Memphis for another hour. Lots of time to talk," the man said, twisting to slide the door home.

The door was yanked from his grip and rolled open with a sharp squeal. Daneeta stood in the aisle.

"Can I help you, sir?" she said, a thin veil of politeness over a well of menace.

"Just visiting," he said turning to her.

Daneeta looked into Merry's pleading eyes.

"No coach passengers allowed in the sleeping cars, sir," she said.

"I was only . . ." the man began, a fresh sheen of sweat on his face.

"No coach passengers allowed in the sleeping cars, sir," she repeated with all the authority of an Amtrak employee and an Old Testament prophet.

She stood aside to allow him into the aisle and watched him shuffle down the narrow corridor back toward the dining car and the coach seats beyond.

"You all right, sweetheart?" Daneeta said.

Merry was shivering. Her fingers ached where she clutched the narrow handle of the butter knife. She made her hand relax. The knife clattered to the compartment's tiled floor.

Merry and Daneeta looked at it lying there at their feet. The attendant stooped and picked up the knife. She looked at Merry and her smile returned. She placed the knife in the pocket of her windbreaker.

"We'll be in Memphis soon. Why don't you come with me up to the dining car and have some hot chocolate until we get there?"

Merry shook her head, eyes welling above a tight smile. "I'd rather stay here."

18

The car revealed nothing. The crime scene guys went over it in situ. Walmart shoppers slowed down to stare at men in bunny suits moving as if they were playing astronaut around the Buick parked in a far corner of the lot near the garden center. It was dusted, vacuumed, scanned and sealed up for towing to a garage behind the Carbondale police building.

It was there that Bill Marquez caught up with it after a wearying drive from Virginia. The two CSI guys gave him the sad news. Lots of prints. Some matched the owner. The rest was anyone's guess. Best guess was an adult male and minor child, possibly female.

"Well, that confirms that we know jack shit," Bill said, eyeing the car with a baleful expression.

"All those hours on the road, the driver had to stop for gas," one tech said.

"And if he had a little girl along they stopped for her to pee a half dozen times," the other tech, father to three daughters, said with deep conviction.

"Yeah, we're pulling in surveillance video from

rest stops, traffic cams and gas stations." Bill took a sip of bitter cop shop coffee. Just what his roiling belly needed after the push from DC.

"He could still be in Carbondale," a local cop offered. "We have a description, such as it is."

"Thanks. But I don't think he's here. He chose a car that would give him a jump on us. One that he knew wouldn't be missed for a long time. My guess is that he's heading far away from here."

"Who is this guy? Did he abduct this kid?" the tech with kids asked.

"Damned if I know. A ghost with all the world to run in and all the money to take him there. And the girl looks like she's along for the ride," Bill said, and tossed the half full cup of coffee into a trash bin.

He found a hotel with rates within bureau standards and checked in. During a long, broiling shower he ran over and over what little he knew. It was like a song he couldn't get out of his head, coming back over and over again to the chorus.

Why Carbondale? Why here? Why leave the car for them to find?

Nancy didn't answer at the office or on her cell. Probably in a meeting.

He lay back on the covers, wrapped in towels and worked forward from what he saw up in Maine days before to the abandoned Buick this morning.

That hooded figure on the convenience store surveillance. The snow still pink with blood where the home invasion crew died. That mother he questioned at Lake Bellevue, what was her name? Danielle Fenton. She wasn't giving up shit. And the ex-wife of Courtland Blanco. There was nothing more she could tell them. He was convinced of that. That bitch would turn in everyone from her grandmother to her first-grade teacher to keep her ass out of a cell.

He drifted off seeing that figure standing at the counter of the Xtra Mart in New Haven. Head bowed, eyes down. Bill dreamt of that man and, in his dreams, the man raised his head to look straight into the camera and his face wasn't the face of a man.

It was the face of a beast.

* * *

He came awake chilled to the bone, the damp towels cold over him and the covers beneath him soaked. The room phone was buzzing. His cell was vibrating across the glass top of the nightstand. He picked up the cell.

"Marquez."

"Wysocki, Homeland. You're in the field on this runner, right?" The gravelly voice of a heavy smoker. Bit of a drawl. Marquez pictured Gary Busey.

"Yeah," Bill said and looked with crusty eyes at the sliver of light coming between the drapes. Was it the same day or had he slept through the night?

"We have a hit in St. Louis. Clear picture eye-dee. Seventy percent match through Perseus."

"Purse-see-us?" Bill said, not sure of what he heard.

"Latest facial recognition program. Got him clear as the cover of People magazine trying to buy tickets to Phoenix using cash. Hundred dollar bills that dinged at Treasury. You need to get that?"

Bill realized the room phone was still buzzing. Probably Nancy to fill him in. It stopped buzzing.

"It's okay. What do you need me to do?" Bill climbed out of bed to enter the bathroom and start the shower. Anything to warm up.

"St. Louis is covering that end for now, canvassing hotels and waiting for the guy to show up for his flight. I need you to get there to take lead. Can you do that?"

"Soon as I get some clothes on, I'm on the road," Bill assured him. The line went dead and he stepped into the warm, steamy embrace of the shower.

* * *

He was still asking himself questions as he tooled along Washington for IL-13. He had a bag of Burger King takeout on the seat by him and a pair of large coffees in the cup holders. It was just after five o'clock. He was running on less than six hours of sleep. Better than nothing.

Getting to St. Louis was going to involve making his way along three different state highways before he reached an interstate far north of Carbondale. The town was isolated, an hour between major highways in any direction. It was as if life, and the interstate highway system, were passing this place by.

So, again, why did Tex, the runner, pick Carbondale to run to?

Watching for signs to lead him to his onramp, he saw one for a train station. He passed the Amtrak station on his left. A couple of hundred yards along he was in the left-hand lane for IL-13. The light turned green and he made a U-turn, pissing off commuters coming off the southbound exit ramp. Horns blared behind him as he pressed the accelerator down to take him back to the train station and the only direct path to anywhere out of Carbondale.

19

A lot of passengers got off the train at Memphis. Daneeta was busy helping an elderly lady with a walker. Merry was able to slip unnoticed back into the coach cars and step off into the platform well away from the sleeper cars at the head of the train.

Merry stood on the open platform with her backpack over her shoulder and her coat in her arms. It was warmer here than in Carbondale. Two men in blue caps and reflective vests were unloading luggage onto carts. People were shuffling toward the station from the coach cars with bags in their hands or rolling cases behind them. One clutch of probably college kids were greeted by friends or relatives. They hugged and laughed. Most passengers just looked tired, grateful the train ride was over.

As she watched and waited for Joyce the crowd on the platform thinned. Only one figure remained, standing by one of the long wooden benches four cars further back.

The man who called himself Axel. He was looking at, watching, Merry.

A conductor spoke into a two-way radio. He held a hand up as Daneeta helped an old couple down out of the car. They were the same ones Merry had seen earlier in the dining car. The woman with the walker. Her husband helped her toward the station.

Daneeta re-entered the car and then exited again to stand looking up and down the platform. Merry stepped behind a concrete support, out of sight of the attendant. She slid to the other side of the column, hugging it.

"Now boarding!" the conductor called. Passengers were filing into the coach cars in a straggling line from the station, lumbering with bags or pulling wheeled cases behind them.

"Now boarding, track three, City of New Orleans," the PA system crackled.

She risked a glance around the corner of the column to see Daneeta speaking to the attendant from another car. The other attendant nodded and shrugged his shoulders. He took tickets from a young couple wearing hiking packs.

Merry looked to where Axel had been standing. He was gone. She looked back to Daneeta who was already up on the steps to the car. She was looking back and forth along the platform. The train started with a jerk and she steadied herself.

Merry felt a pang at the thought of Daneeta eventually finding her gone from her cabin. She imagined the frantic search aboard the train; a sick feeling twisted her stomach. It felt wrong. So many things felt wrong since she'd left Huntsville with her father last year. She tried to think of it all as an adventure, like she was a spy on a mission in a hostile country. Only none of it felt like pretend play. It felt like lying and mean tricks. She almost ran back onto the platform to let Daneeta see her but remembered her father's trust in her to follow his instructions.

As the train rumbled back to life to move from the station, Merry hurried away from the platform, following the old couple toward the ramp leading into the station. The old man was holding a door open for the woman. The door swung shut as Merry reached it and shouldered inside.

A hand touched her arm. She made to pull away and the touch became a grip.

Axel's hand encircled her arm. He looked down at her, his lips wet. He was taller than she remembered, rangy with sloped shoulders.

"You need a ride home, huh?" he said.

She drew away but his hold tightened until it hurt her arm. He stepped in closer.

"Just tell me where you live and I'll take you there. I know every street in Memphis," he said and turned to yank her along with him. He was pulling her along, tucked close to his side. Her sneakers squeaked on the tiles as she dragged her feet. He jerked her upright hard enough to make her gasp. She fell into step with him.

Her father told her never to go anywhere with strangers. He told her that Gunny taught him that no matter how bad things get, wherever strangers wanted to take you they'll only get worse.

Merry shut her eyes and drew in her breath. She clamped her jaws tight and drew up her shoulders. The loudest, shrillest scream she could imagine was welling up from her belly.

The vise on her arm was released with a suddenness that made her stumble. She opened her eyes to see Joyce taking her hand, gently.

"Sorry, Merry. Ran into traffic," Joyce said, smiling. "My truck's out this way."

They moved toward the doors and the sunshine outside. Merry glanced back. Axel was down on his knees holding his stomach. His face was white as a fish belly. His glasses lay in a puddle of puke spreading over the marble floor.

"What did you do to him?" Merry asked with more curiosity than compassion.

"I was a Marine, too, Merry. A woman in a man's world. I picked up a trick or two."

"Can you teach me how to do that?"

"You really want to learn?" Joyce said.

Merry nodded with enthusiasm.

"Well then, you and me are going to get along just fine." Joyce put her arm around the little girl and hurried them both to the parking lot.

20

Mansoor noticed the minute the big guy walked into Kay-Cee Auto Parts. Canvas winter coat. Work boots. The guy was walking the aisles idly. Most customers came right to the back counter because most people didn't know what the fuck they're looking for. Mansoor was helping a customer with air filters for a Toyota. Maria, his sister, was finishing up a tire order.

The big guy spent time looking through a display of fan belts, his back to the counter. The customer buying tires made up his mind and Maria took his credit card. Mansoor found the air filter for a '08 Corolla in stock and let Maria ring that up too. Then he sent her to the McDonald's for coffee.

Once the store was empty but for himself and big guy Mansoor asked, "Can I do something for you?"

"I'm looking to sell a truck. '14 Tahoe. It's loaded," the big guy said when he reached the counter.

"This look like a dealership to you? Try Craig's List."

"I don't have any papers on it. I was looking for

a quick sale. I'm new in Kansas City." The big guy stood, hands on the counter, eyes unblinking.

"I don't know anyone looking to buy a Tahoe."

"I'm talking a good price. Fast cash."

Mansoor studied the guy. Mostly his hands. Rough hands that had seen work. The skin on his face had seen a lot of sun at one point. And there was a set to the eyes, something hard.

"You're not a cop, 'cause this would be entrapment," Mansoor said, tapping the counter with his fingers.

"You know anyone looking for a deal?"

Mansoor reached over to a wire steel rack that rested on the counter. He plucked a business card from one of the pockets and slid it over the counter.

"Ask for Khaled. And don't take his first offer."

"Who do I say sent me?"

"Nobody sent you. Just go," Mansoor said and watched until the big guy was out the door and off the front lot in a salt-streaked Tahoe.

* * *

The satellite phone trilled on the seat beside him.

Levon picked it up as he drove down St. John Avenue in the North Indian Mound neighborhood of Kansas City. It was trying to snow. The wipers smeared fallen flakes across the windscreen.

"That you, honey?" he said.

"It's me, Daddy." Merry's voice on the other end. "Joyce and I are driving back to Gunny's cabin."

"Did you like your train ride?"

"It was okay." Her voice was subdued. She was still raw over the sudden separation.

"You'll have fun. You talk all the time about visiting Gunny and Joyce."

"I know. I thought it would be both of us."

"It's only for a little while, honey."

"Then where will we go?"

"I've been thinking about that. There are a few possibilities I'm working on."

"Okay." An empty response.

"No more cheap hotels and take-out. I promise."

"Okay." Even more vacant this time.

"Tell Joyce to call me when she isn't driving."

"Okay. Bye, Daddy."

He dropped the phone to the seat beside him and looked for All-Town Towing and Haul.

* * *

"I'll give you three grand cash," Khaled Maloof said, stepping away from the Tahoe parked on a lot behind his garage. The building was a block structure with a steel roof overhang. Flatbed haulers and tow trucks came and went. A long row of rental vans lined the fence at the back of the property.

"How about in trade?" Levon said.

Khaled squinted at him. "Trade? Trade what? A lifetime of tows?"

"I need papers. Good ones."

"Let's go for a ride," Khaled said. "Wait here."

He went into the office and returned with keys for one of the rental vans. He motioned Levon to get in the passenger side of an Econoline.

When they were well away from the garage, Khaled asked, "The papers. How good?" He was piloting the van along quiet streets lined with single homes, the lawns blanketed in white from the recent snowfall. The sidewalks were shoveled and salted.

"Top quality. A set for me and a set for a female minor. Passport for me. Driver's license. Utility bills. Social security numbers. Good ones. Solid ones."

"What you're asking for, that Tahoe won't even cover ten points. You know that?"

"Consider it a deposit to get the process started. Make introductions. Can you help me?"

"I know people who can."

"Then the Tahoe is your finder's fee."

"I'll see what I can do. How can I reach you?"

"I'm at the Holiday Inn on Prairie Crossing. Know it?"

"Near Schlitterbahn? What name?"

"Matthew Dresher. You can drop me there. The Tahoe's yours."

Khaled hooked a right at the next light to take them to the highway west to the Parallel Parkway. The six-lane gleamed under a fresh sheen of salt melt. Trucks hissed by them off the access ramp as they sped up to slide into the flow.

"How'd you find me? Or did you pull into the first Muslim-owned place you came to, figuring we're all bent?"

"I went to a Chaldean first."

Khaled laughed.

He snorted. "Who was it? Hanna over at the Goodyear? Or that shit Mansoor? Whoever it was didn't trust you enough to send you to another Assyrian."

"I promised I wouldn't say."

Khaled laughed harder.

"It was Mansoor then. Hanna would want me to know it was him fucking me. Don't worry. Doesn't matter. It's all good. So you know Chaldeans from

Muslims. You didn't learn that on TV."

Levon said nothing.

"You know something. You were somewhere to learn what you know. I won't ask. You only want to do business. I only want to do business. The guys I'll send to you, they are all business."

"That's all I'm looking for," Levon said.

Khaled drove onto the Holiday Inn lot and stopped under the awning before the entrance.

"Matthew Dresher, right? You want to leave a number?" Khaled said as Levon stepped out of the van.

"They can ask for me at the desk. I'll come down," Levon said. He walked for the entrance, the doors sliding open to admit him.

Khaled pulled back onto the parkway. He thumbed his cell phone. It rang three times before a sleepy voice answered.

"Jerry? I'm looking for your useless uncle," he said in Arabic.

21

"The guy has craft. He's a player. He has to be in the system somewhere," Bill Marquez said.

"You were told to take lead in St. Louis." The tobacco-ravaged voice of Wysocki of DHS growled in his ear. The man was annoyed.

"But we dropped a thread here in Carbondale," Bill insisted. He was in the closet-cramped Amtrak security office on the second floor of the Carbondale station building. The single security officer had given up the office when Bill showed his FBI ID.

"Tell me."

"He picked this town because it has an Amtrak station. I went over surveillance video at the station from last night. I found him buying a round trip ticket to San Antonio, Texas. I have a crystal clear shot of him at the sales counter."

Bill was looking at the footage on a monitor before him. He could see Roeder, Tex, Bruckman, whoever, standing at the ticket counter handing over his ID and cash. The camera set to one side of the booth caught him in painful detail. A second monitor showed the platform from a high angle, the subject standing with a little girl until a train rolled into the station. The subject spoke to a train attendant before the girl boarded. Tex stood watching the train depart before walking from the platform and back into the station.

"One we didn't catch on Perseus?"

"That's what I'm telling you. He has a beard in this footage. And he's wearing Band-Aids on his ear lobes. He disguised the line of his jaw and the shape of his ears. He did that to fool the facial recognition filters. He didn't want us to find him buying those tickets."

"He's on a train then?"

"No, that's just it," Bill said. "He bought the tickets in cash using a new ID. Oscar Bruckman. I'll send you a scan of that. But the tickets are in the name Megan Elizabeth Bruckman. The girl he's traveling with."

"They've split up. We can find the little girl but it's him we want," Wysocki said.

"Or it's a feint. Something to throw us off."

"How so?"

"We picked him up on video in St. Louis. Clear as day. He goes to a place where he knows practically his every move will be covered in high-def. He makes sure we see him. He pays in cash using a bullshit photo ID that he knows will raise red flags. And the Band-Aids are gone. And he's shaved. He wants us to know he's in St. Louis, think he's in St. Louis."

"Why would he want us to think that?" Wysocki was hooked now, the edge in his voice gone.

"So that we spend a day looking for him in St.

Louis. And we waste manpower staking out the airport tomorrow waiting for him to take that flight. He doesn't plan on showing up."

"Then where is he? If you're right, he most likely got back on the road. To where?"

"I don't know that yet," Bill said. "But we know that girl is on that train. And we know he's doing his damnedest to lead us away from her."

"I have the scan and the video you sent. Easy enough to find out where that train is," Wysocki said. Bill could hear tapping keys in the background and rising voices. The shit had been stirred.

"Where do you want me, sir?"

"Hang tight where you are, Marquez. I'll have someone get back to you. Five minutes. Good work on this."

The line went dead.

* * *

Bill had the front seat of the bureau car reclined and the heater turned up to the max. He was catching a few minutes of relative peace in the station's parking lot when his cell buzzed. It was Wysocki.

"I still want you in St. Louis to take lead. There's someone on the way to you to take over there on follow-up. Something in St. Louis should give us an idea of what direction this guy took."

"And the girl?"

"The train's next stop is New Orleans. I have agents there waiting for it. We'll take her into custody and see who she is and what she can tell us."

"Is anyone looking for cars stolen here in Carbondale? What did he use to get to St. Louis?"

"Ahead of you on that. We have a '13 Chrysler reported stolen from near you that turned up illegally parked at the St. Louis airport. It's in impound with a hands-off order on it. A team's en route to sweep it."

"That means he has another ride by now," Bill said, knuckling his eyes. He spared a look in the mirror above the dash. His eyes looked like he'd dashed Tabasco in them.

Wysocki said, "We seized the cash he used to buy the plane tickets to Phoenix. The Fed has the scans as of an hour ago. ATF has someone on the scene. What about the cash he used to buy the train tickets?"

"I told the Amtrak office here to hold their deposit until tomorrow. They weren't happy about it. Can anyone go through the bills here?"

"Treasury's sending someone from St. Louis. You'll probably pass them on your way there. How are you holding up?"

"A little ragged, sir. I've been on the move since this thing broke."

"You'll have time to rack out in the back seat. The agents I'm sending will do the driving."

Two hours of sleep cramped in a moving car. Like a vacation in Maui, Bill thought.

"Thank you, sir."

"Make it 'Darren.' You're on the team now," Wysocki said and broke the connection.

Bill tossed his phone onto the seat by him and dropped his head back on the rest. Their subject was in the wind, adios, but leaving a trail of crumbs for them to find. It was obvious he was leading them away from the girl. They'd have her soon enough. What would she know about where Tex was heading? The guy already showed that he could appear and disappear at will. Breaking off from the little girl, someone he obviously cared about, might mean he was making a last goodbye, a run for the border and oblivion.

And who the hell was this guy? Most crooks were stupid. Even the smart ones got dumber when they tried to run. And the longer they were on the run the dumber, more careless they got. Not Tex. This guy stayed cool, deliberate. He was relying on skills that were trained into him. He was hardwired for escape and evasion and now he had freed himself of all encumbrances for a final vanishing act.

In addition to knowing how to run and hide, the guy was a stone killer as well. All on his own he took down a crew whose history read like a horror movie. He skated across a dozen states with a minor child in tow. If the cash he was spending wasn't so red-hot the feds would still be up in Maine scratching their asses.

But how is a guy like that not in the system? Prints, nada. Picture, nada. He wasn't a foreign national. Only a born American who understood the nuances could game his way this far.

So who was Tex?

A rap on the window by his head brought him bolt upright. Somewhere in his thoughts he'd fallen hard asleep. A face in the window smiled an apology. The face was ruddy with the cold. A man in a black raincoat with a second, slighter man standing beside another bureau car pulled up alongside.

"You Marquez?" the ruddy face man said.

Bill stepped from the car. "Bill Marquez."

"I'm Tom Doolin. This is Tom Salucci. We're your ride to St. Lou."

"Tom and Tom." Bill smiled weakly. The cold air

was like a slap to exposed skin on his face and hands.

"Maybe last names would be better," Doolin said, face creased with an open smile.

"What about this car?" Bill said as he hauled his bag from the back seat.

"Somebody's coming to get it. Leave the keys under the floor mat." Doolin took the bag and handed it off to Salucci who popped the trunk and placed it inside.

"Back seat's all yours," Doolin said with a grin and held the door for him.

Bill stretched out as best he could, knees bent against the front passenger seat. He felt the car sway under him as it backed from the parking space. They hit the road, tires swishing. He vowed only to close his eyes for a minute. But soon the hiss of the wiper blades turned to the whisper of surf over white sand and he was lying in the sun on a beach atop a blanket of crisp hundred dollar bills.

22

He met the pair in the lobby of the Holiday Inn. They stood waiting for him by a gurgling fountain, eyes on the bank of elevators. They wore black leather car coats. Olive complexions. One was thickly bearded with a gut hanging over his belt; the other was lean with a bristling mustache. They wore permanent scowls, eyes hard.

"I'm Dresher," Levon said by way of identification rather than an introduction.

"We have a car out front," the lean one said. No discernible accent other than flat Midwest.

He followed them out to a Mercury where a driver waited with the engine running. Levon got into the back seat with lean one. The beard took the passenger seat. A woman in a headscarf was driving. She glanced back at him in the rearview before pulling from the curb. Black eyes studied him with a cold light.

"We drive around a while," the lean one said and settled back in his seat.

Levon said nothing. They'd make sure they

weren't tailed. And taking a switchback route to their destination would have the added benefit of disorienting him. He watched out his window at the moon moving behind powerlines and over rooftops.

They entered a warren of streets lined with the dark faces of rowhomes set back from tiny front yards lumpy with snow. They turned left then right then left again, never following a street for more than a few blocks. The woman drove without direction from the men in the car. They'd either discussed the route beforehand or left it to the driver.

The man by Levon said something to the passenger in the front seat. They spoke in low tones accented with grunts. Mesopotamian Arabic. They were Iraqi. The lean one glanced at Levon to see if he was listening. Levon sat watching the moon.

Satisfied that the white guy couldn't understand, the lean one asked in Arabic, "Is Ghadeer back from California?"

"He said he was staying another day," the beard said.

"Does Danny know that?"

"I don't know. Should we tell him?"

"And listen to his shit? Ghadeer is his cousin. That makes it his problem."

Just idle chatter. Levon listened, recalling names only. It sounded like Danny was the one in charge. He'd be the one they were going to now.

The lean one said something to the woman and she turned right at the next corner, went straight a few blocks to cross a bright street lined with storefronts. A dry cleaner on a corner, a blue neon sign reading Rite-Wash. The streets behind were dark. The road they were on curved past dim streets of single homes through trees growing close by the road before opening up to flat expanses of snow covered fields. A high cyclone fence raced by them along the right. Levon could see pole lights illuminating long featureless buildings.

The car turned into a driveway and up to a gate. The driver's window rolled down half way. Icy air knifed in through the gap. The woman reached an arm through the open window to punch a series of numbers into a keypad on a metal stanchion. Levon noted the sequence. Six. Four. Four. Nine.

She rolled the window back up. The double-wide gate swung slowly inward. The driveway inside the fence had not been recently plowed. The tires crunched over a few inches of snow, treads mashing down the hard frost crust. The headlights showed the hard outlines of ruts ahead of them. Several cars or trucks had entered or exited since the last snowfall.

The car pulled past a row of steel cargo containers and stopped in a pool of light between two long steel structures lined with garage doors. The driver touched the tab of a remote clipped to the sun visor. A garage door crept open, a bar of yellow light growing beneath it. When it was fully open she pulled inside to park by a Mercedes sedan sitting in a puddle of fresh snow melt.

The lean one said, "We're here," and motioned for Levon to exit.

The driver remained behind the wheel while the men stepped out into the open warehouse area. There were rows of boxes shrink-wrapped atop pallets. Some were appliances like microwave ovens or computers. Others were cartons marked with unreadable lettering stamped on them and contents stickers. A forklift sat recharging, a long cable stretching back into the dark recesses of the building.

The lean one and the beard guided him to the door of a low structure against the back wall. It was the size of a double-wide trailer. Light came through the windows from behind blinds. The lean one pulled a door open and motioned Levon inside.

Rather than the office he expected, Levon was surprised to find the room looked more like a suite from a casino hotel. Or at least a cheaper version of one. Thick carpeting, plush furniture in crushed velvet, blood red and pumpkin orange. A long wall of mirrors tinted bronze. A basketball game played muted on a big screen television mounted on a wall paneled in faux cherry wood. A broad marble-topped coffee table held a sand-filled ashtray at the center. At one end was a tidy kitchenette with granite countertops and white cabinets. A second door led to what Levon presumed was a bathroom. The room smelled of cologne and stale tobacco smoke.

A man sat with his back to them, puffing a cigar and speaking on a cell phone. Levon noted a neat row of six identical phones arrayed on the table top.

"You sent me shit so I pay you shit," the cigar smoker said in Arabic. "You bring me better then I pay you better. Or maybe I pay someone else. It is business. We can do business my way or not at all. Try to understand that."

The smoker ended the call by hurling the phone across the room.

"Eli far ab t'zak!" he growled to himself before turning to greet his guests. A predator leer replaced his expression of contempt at the caller. The cigar wobbled in his clenched teeth.

"Danny Safar. You're looking for good eye-dee?" the smoker said, standing and offering his hand. He was a man in his fifties. Once fit and going to fat.

"Matt Dresher." Levon took the man's hand. There was power there. Safar stood a head shorter than him but had broad shoulders and thick arms that stretched the fabric of his open twill shirt.

Safar nodded, meeting Levon's eyes. "Is that who you are or who you want to be?"

"It's who I am for now. You're going to tell me who I'm going to be next, right?"

Safar grunted at that, amused. He turned to Levon's escorts and spoke in flat Arabic. "You were not followed?"

"We came through Armourdale. Took our time. No one was behind us," the lean one said.

"He's not wired?"

The lean one bit his lip. The beard shrugged.

"Jerry!" Safar called, eyes still hard on Levon's escorts.

He turned to the door at the far end of the room and called the name again, louder.

Levon heard a toilet flush followed by water running. A young man emerged from the bathroom. Shaved head. A black running suit with yellow stripes on the legs and sleeves. His eyes were bloodshot and face flushed. The flesh around one of his eyes was yellowed and the lids were puffy. Jerry was recovering from either a recent fight or a recent beatdown.

"Yes, uncle?" Jerry said.

"The thing. Get the thing," Safar said with impatience, returning to English. He waved open hands at Levon in a gesture like an amateur magician.

"You need to learn how to work these things yourself." Jerry rummaged in a cabinet to retrieve a voltage reader.

"I have you for that," Safar said and stood aside for Jerry to step up to Levon with the bright yellow wand.

Levon removed his coat and raised his arms from his sides to stand with his feet shoulder-width apart. The young man moved the wand over his back, chest, belly and crotch. Levon lifted his untucked shirt to reveal the Sig Sauer snug in his waistband.

"Did you even know he had that?" Safar said in Arabic, cutting his eyes toward the escorts. They shuffled and mumbled replies.

"Is the gun a problem?" Levon said.

"I only wanted to know it was there," Safar said, shrugging.

"Nothing. No batteries. No reading," Jerry said, stepping back.

"Now we do business," Safar said.

23

Jerry couldn't take his eyes off the diamonds.

Uncle Danny left the Wasem brothers to channel surf his big screen. He ordered Jerry to make them coffee.

Now his uncle sat with the white guy at the table in the kitchenette. The white guy had taken a paper envelope from his coat pocket and spilled the contents onto the table top in a tiny heap. A dozen cut diamonds glittered. The largest was the size of a pistachio nut.

"What is this?" his uncle said, waving a hand over the glittering pile.

"These aren't traceable. Cash is. These are better than cash," the white guy said.

"I don't know diamonds," his uncle said and pursed his lips as he poked a finger into the pile, separating the gems.

"Then take them to someone who does. I need to start the process here. You take the stones. Have them valued. If they aren't worth what I'm asking for then I don't get what I want." The white guy sat back.

Jerry placed two cups of strong black coffee in front of the men. His eyes took in the diamonds. They cast constellations of white reflections on the table top. They looked real enough to him.

"You trust me with them?" his uncle said, hand hovering over the table, eyes on the white guy.

"I want you to trust me. At least enough to get my papers started."

"Okay." Uncle Danny picked each stone up to return it to the envelope.

"So, we're good?"

"We're good," Danny said and snapped his fingers at his nephew. "Get a paper and pen."

Danny dictated a Haskell Avenue address and the white guy wrote it down in neat block letters.

"Go to that address in the morning. They'll know you're coming. Tell them what you need and we'll see if these gems cover the cost."

"I think you'll be pleased," the white guy said.

"Get him a phone," Danny said.

Jerry opened a drawer filled with a dozen identical cell phones. He chose one. After recording the number on his own phone he handed it to the white guy.

"Jerry will stay in touch with you. Only Jerry. Only use the phone to answer calls from us. When our business is done you give us back the phone. Is this clear to you?"

The white guy nodded and pocketed the phone. Danny returned to Arabic, calling to the Wasem brothers who were lounging in the fat chairs, critiquing the porno movie they'd settled on.

"Take this asshole back. Watch his hotel to make sure he has no visitors."

"How long do we watch?" the beard said.

"Until I call you. Then I have something else for you to do," Uncle Danny said, brushing a hand toward them in a shooing gesture.

Jerry watched the white guy who sat sipping coffee, his face betraying nothing.

He set the cup down when the Wasems stood and called to him. He followed them from the warehouse.

"You think he's for real, uncle?" Jerry said, making to sit at the table until his uncle's scowl made him stand again.

"If the diamonds are real then he is real. What cop pays that way? They always offer shitty money. Drug money."

"What do you think they are worth?"

"I know diamonds? I know shit about diamonds. I'll take them to a Jew. He'll tell me they're worth half of what they are worth and offer me half of that for them. And if it's enough for me I will be happy to be rid of them."

"I could make a better deal maybe," Jerry offered. "A Lebanese I know owns a couple of jewelry stores."

"A Lebanese? Worse than a Jew. And how would I know you'd bring the money back?" His uncle rose, carrying the coffee into the entertainment area and sitting down.

Jerry raised a hand to touch the fading bruise around his eye. It was still tender to the touch. A week ago it had been swollen shut. Jerry had skimmed a little off a pay run to buy some coke. The plan was to turn the coke into more cash and replace what he'd skimmed. Instead, he took the four ounces of powder on a long weekend in Vegas with his girlfriend. When Monday came the coke was gone, sucked up by some brand new friends they'd invited to a party in their room. Jerry came back with no coke and no money to replace what he'd "borrowed."

Uncle Danny was not understanding. Uncle Danny had no sympathy for youthful enthusiasm. Uncle Danny had spent his youthful enthusiasm in Saddam's army fighting the Iranians.

Jerry was given a thorough working over by the Wasem brothers. Not hard enough to put him in the hospital but hard enough to make him piss pink for a couple of weeks. One of the Wasems, Khalid, the fat one, delivered the fist to Jerry's eye. They had been under strict orders not to because Uncle Danny did not wish to hear about it from Jerry's mother who was Danny's little sister. So Jerry was staying close by his uncle until the bruising went away. That meant doing woman's chores like errands and making coffee.

"Now, get this shit off my television," Uncle Danny commanded and waggled a hand toward the enthusiastic women writhing naked on his big screen.

Jerry plucked the remote from the sofa and switched the TV back to ESPN. He did every menial task for his uncle, even working the remote control easily within reach of his uncle's hand.

It won't always be this way, he thought as he returned to the kitchenette to take the white guy's cup to the sink.

All I need is one break. Just watch for one break so I can make my own deal. Have my own crew. Stop being Uncle Danny's bitch, he thought, rinsing the coffee cup and returning it to its hook like a good wife.

Maybe this white guy was the break he was looking for. The man was on the run. Financing his getaway with stolen swag. He wouldn't spend it all on a phony driver's license and credit card. He'd have more somewhere.

Jerry dried his hands on a paper towel before removing his cell from his pocket. He looked at Matt Dresher's number on the screen.

His eye didn't hurt so much now.

24

The girl wasn't on the train when it reached New Orleans.

The train was delayed for four hours in Yazoo City when an attendant found her cabin empty an hour out of Memphis. Every car was searched and the girl was not found. The disappearance of a minor child traveling alone on one of their trains sent a shiver of terror up the corporate spine of Amtrak. Local and state police were called in both in Mississippi and Tennessee. The area around Memphis station was searched for evidence as was the station in Greenwood, the only stop before Yazoo. An Amber Alert was sent out over four states.

The only agency not called in was the FBI who had agents waiting throughout the day at Union Passenger Terminal in New Orleans to question Megan Elizabeth Bruckman when she detrained.

State CID reviewed the video footage in Memphis based on account of an eyewitness who told them about a strange man she saw pestering the child just before the stop there. The highly stressed train attendant told them that a coach passenger had entered the sleeping cars to talk to the girl. This was corroborated by a waiter in the dining car who gave the same description of a tall man in his thirties. Dark hair. Glasses. Creepy. Both the attendant and waiter used that last word.

The video footage from the platform clearly showed the man identified by the train crew detraining in Memphis. Shortly after, the Bruckman girl exited the train carrying a backpack. Two different angles showed the "creepy guy" watching the girl from concealment and following her into the station.

The "creepy" passenger was quickly identified from the train's manifest as Axel Louis Colfax.

It was eight in the evening when a tactical team of combined Memphis PD and staties hammered down the front and rear doors of the Colfax home, startling his elderly parents. Axel was found playing Super Mario in a room the cops at first assumed belonged to much younger sibling until they learned that Axel was an only child. The suspect appeared to be either ill or high on some controlled substance. A further search of the home failed to uncover evidence of a missing child.

The search did uncover a locked room in the basement. Their warrant gave them all latitude in their search and so the lock was snipped with bolt cutters and the room was entered by a half dozen cops calling Megan's name. Instead of the allegedly abducted girl, either dead or alive, the cops found a treasure trove of child pornography lovingly boxed and filed by subject matter. A computer and CPU towers promised even more.

It was swiftly determined that all of this was evidence relating to a suspected abduction. Axel Colfax was a registered sex offender and therefore, by his past actions, stripped of many of his constitutional rights. The presumption of innocence was strained to the point where they could haul him in. The boxes and hard drives were carted off along with Axel. Flashes fired from police cameras backed up the damning evidence caught by the body-cams each cop wore.

Further viewing of video footage from Memphis Amtrak Station exonerated Colfax when it was clearly proven that he did not leave the station with the little girl.

High definition footage taken from a camera set high on one of the station's fluted columns plainly showed Colfax bracing the Bruckman girl only to see them both approached by an adult female of undetermined age. This female took Colfax to the floor with two lightning fast actions that made even the hardened state CID cops wince in empathy. The woman had moves. Colfax was left puking his guts out and searching for his testicles which were probably residing somewhere north of his navel after the ass-whupping received from the unidentified female. The female was then seen walking hand-in-hand from the station with the child identified as the Bruckman girl.

The mystery was solved for the arresting officers as to why the suspect Colfax was seated holding a bag of crushed ice on his crotch. Colfax was cleared of abduction charges but held on the shitload of violations of his sex offender status represented by the vast library of kiddie rape photos, videos, and comic books found in his basement lair in boxes and on his hard drive.

For all of this law enforcement action, the feds in New Orleans were not looped in. They were left to question the train staff already exhausted from the grilling they'd received in Yazoo.

Team Megan, the section of the task force assigned with identifying, finding and questioning the minor person of interest, shifted focus to Memphis.

Team Roeder, a combined unit of Bureau and Treasury tasked with finding the adult male fugitive, was left to spread out all over the lower Midwest chasing shadows.

The following morning, the Feds, TSA and local cops staking out the departures in St. Louis waited two hours past the take-off of the nine-thirty to Phoenix. Matthew Dresher was a no-show.

Everyone turned to Bill Marquez, acting lead in St. Louis. His prediction that the airport stakeout would result in a big zero came true. Beyond that he had no answers. Tex had an overnight jump on them. He could be anywhere in eight states—if he was still on the ground. Anywhere in the world if he managed to get airborne somehow.

Gone into the ether with the key to a multi-billion dollar fortune.

25

"Do you know what this is?" Gunny asked, turning the flash drive in his fingers.

"All Daddy told me was that you should hide it," Merry said.

They were snug in the cabin's kitchen. It was dark outside, forest dark. A freezing rain pattered on the windows. The branches of the trees looked like they were encased in glass. Joyce made coffee for herself and Gunny. Hot chocolate for Merry along with a plate of oatmeal raisin cookies baked from a roll of dough Joyce kept in the chest freezer.

"Levon didn't tell you what's on it?" Joyce asked. She plucked the drive from Gunny's hand and detached the silver chain.

"No. He found it in Maine in someone's house. He said it's important."

"He wouldn't be asking me to watch over it if it weren't," Gunny said. "Must be his ace in the hole."

"What's that?" Merry asked.

"It's a card you don't play until you have to," Gunny said.

"That means it's something someone wants. Someone could come looking." Joyce took Gunny's hand to drop the plastic lozenge in his open palm.

"I'll make sure they don't find it. I'll hide it in a place only a blind man would think of," Gunny said.

* * *

Levon called the following morning.

He spoke to Gunny first.

"The drive has bank account numbers and names on it along with passwords. The government will be looking for it for sure. I don't know who else might be interested. That little thumb drive could be worth a billion dollars."

"I don't need to know what it is. I only need to know that it's important to you," Gunny said, standing in the morning chill with the sat phone to his ear.

"Only fair that you know what you're hiding. That you know the value and the risk."

"Roger that. Your little girl is here safe. She's having breakfast with Joyce. What are your plans, son?"

"Break contact. Charlie Mike." Continue mission.

"Good luck, marine."

"Can you put Merry on, Gunny?"

Gunny and Joyce sat in the kitchen while Merry stood by the bay window in the great room and spoke in a low voice with her father. She was looking out at the crystalline wonder of the ice-rimed forest. The girl returned to the kitchen after a while. Her eyes and nose were red but she fought to keep a smile on her face. She placed the sat phone on the table by Gunny.

"My daddy wants you to hide the phone. Mine too. He said the next time we see him it'll be in person. He'll come for me when it's safe."

Gunny placed his hand atop Merry's.

"And he will, honey. That man keeps his word. Come hell, high water or the wrath of God, that man only ever says what he means."

"I'm not hungry anymore. May I go lay down?"

"You sure can. You're still tired from that long day yesterday," Joyce said, fighting to keep her tone light.

Merry left the kitchen to go to the den that Joyce had set up as a guest room.

Joyce made to rise from the table. Gunny took her wrist in his hand.

"I know you want to go to her."

"She's hurting, Gunny. She's scared." Joyce sat down and patted Gunny's hand until he released her.

"And that's not going to change until her daddy comes through that door. She doesn't need to be babied. You just let her have a good cry."

"She's not one of your jarheads," Joyce said, but she said it in a kind way.

"Sure she is. And she's tough enough to make it through the Crucible on Parris Island. She's got a lot of her Daddy in her blood," Gunny said.

After coffee, Gunny took the flash drive and the pair of satellite phones deep into the woods. He didn't come back until almost noon. Joyce had a fire in the fireplace and lunch waiting for him. Merry came out to join them.

Nothing was said about where he went or how long he'd been gone.

After wolfing down half a grilled cheddar cheese and sun-dried tomato sandwich, Merry asked, "Are there any books here I can read?"

"I have a Kindle you can use. We can download

some books on there," Joyce offered.

"Cool," Merry said, setting to work on the second half of her sandwich.

Gunny beamed an "I told you so" smile in the direction of Joyce's voice.

She aimed an exaggerated wince back at him. He couldn't see it but she knew he could feel it.

> Gunny Leffertz said:
> *"Always have a plan. And always expect that plan to get fucked in the ass."*

26

Levon arrived at the address given him by Danny
Safar. It was a music store in a pokey strip mall. The
sign out front promised music lessons "taught by
professionals." The store was empty except for the
gray-haired man in a ragged cardigan behind the
counter.

"This way," the man said and led Levon past racks
of guitars to one of three doors in the rear of the
store. He opened the door and gestured for Levon
to enter.

The room was set up for music practice. A stand
in the middle of the room and three chairs. The only
feature on the walls was a faded print: a painting of
a young girl playing the violin in an idyllic pastoral
setting with woodland animals seated about atten-
tively listening.

"Stand against that wall. I'll be right back," the
man said and left the room. Levon removed his
winter coat and stood with his back to the wall in a
pale green work shirt.

The man returned with a camera and tripod.

"Smile if you want to," the man said, standing on his tiptoes to look through the lens level with Levon's face. Levon relaxed his face to appear as harmless as possible. He attempted a half smile.

A half dozen clicks of the shutter and they were done. They exited the room. The man went behind the counter to secure the camera and tripod somewhere out of sight.

"You have something for me?" the man said.

Levon handed over his wish list. Two different driver's licenses under two different names. Auto insurance cards to match each. An immunization form for Merry. Two utility bills under a name matching one of the licenses. A working credit card to be used for ID only. Birth certificates for both of them. He included their vital information for those. Date of birth, hair color, eye color. He also indicated that they'd need these new identities to originate from locales somewhere well below the Mason-Dixon line. They could fake a lot of things but there was no getting past his and Merry's southern drawls, syntax, and vocabulary.

The man in the cardigan looked over the paper, written on three sheets of Holiday Inn stationary in neat rows of block letters.

"An expensive list," the man said, eyes lifted to look at Levon.

"Does my payment cover it?" Levon said.

"You're covered. Were you expecting change?" A flicker of a smile. A joke. Or half a joke.

"No. When can I expect all that?"

"Give me two days. Someone will contact you."

The brass bell hung above the door tinkled a merry tone. A woman entered ushering a child with a guitar case ahead of her.

"Okay then," Levon said and left the store.

* * *

The burner cell charged and in his coat pocket, Levon was free to roam. Spending all day at the hotel was a bad idea. Staying in one place was not an option. Safar's crew knew where to find him. That had to change.

He'd paid three days ahead for the room at the Holiday Inn. That's where they'd expect him to be. Early the next morning, he left the hotel unseen and made his way down the Parallel Parkway to a Motel 8 and checked in using cash. A week in advance and no housekeeping. The clerk, a woman with limp yellow hair and sad eyes, didn't ask questions.

From there he walked to a strip mall anchored by a Kmart. Most of the stores weren't open yet. He ate breakfast at a Bob Evans and waited.

At the Kmart he bought sweats, a pair of running shoes and a bag of socks. He stopped by a Mail Boxes Etc. and paid in cash for a mailbox large enough to receive parcels. He paid two months in advance. He also bought a book of stamps and some padded envelopes.

Back at the Motel 8 he changed into the sweats, sneakers and his hooded jacket and went for a run. He moved at an even pace along the parkway shoulder. His run took him past churches, a hospital and car dealerships. At the entrance to Schlitterbahn he hooked a left to run the ring road around the massive water park, now closed for the season. Signs, starkly colorful in the gray winter light, promised a reopening in May.

He ran along the fence, pushing himself to a sprint. Sucking down the chilled air. Feeling the blood fill the muscles of his legs and shoulders. His world became the run; the long stretch and shallow curves ahead of him. This was a place he could count on to remain constant. No matter where he found himself in the world, the mountains of Helmand, the desert of Iraq, the jungles of Colombia, the run was the same. His endurance against the elements, fatigue and age.

A flat out run up the entrance road brought him back to the parkway, muscles burning and lungs ablaze. He slowed to a jog and continued west, only slowing in the shadow of the 435 overpass. He paused there, jogging in place. Gradually sloping concrete banks lined either side of the roadway leading up the supports that held up the span and the traffic thundering by above. Set in the banks were lengths of steel hoops that served as handholds for road maintenance workers or inspectors to reach the understructure of the bridges.

Levon turned then and jogged back the way he came, falling to a walking pace for the final three miles to the Motel 8.

27

"Your friend isn't answering," the geek behind the Holiday Inn desk said with a simpering smile.

"He's still here, right?" Jerry Safar said, going red in the face.

"He's paid through Friday."

"Probably in the shower. I could just go up and knock on his door."

"It's against Holiday Inn policy to give out our guests' room numbers," the geek said and gave a little shoulder roll in apology as he replaced the phone in its dock.

"Shit," Jerry said and stepped away from the counter to make way for a family of four dragging luggage across the lobby.

He slid behind the wheel of the Mercedes S-Class he'd left running at the entryway.

"Shit," he said again and gunned from under the portico.

* * *

The sign out front of Glitters promised "all-naked

girls."

Inside a single dancer moved out of time to Carrie Underwood. She was certainly all-naked if a number of years past being a girl. Even low lights and some skilled surgery failed to conceal that fact. But it was early afternoon and the place was mostly empty, the seats around the stage entirely so. The customers in the booths were here to drink not ogle.

Jerry came to do business in the private booth he called his "office" when it wasn't being used for lap dances. He coaxed Taz Uzon away from the door for his pitch. Taz was a bouncer and some relation to the owner of Glitters, a Turk named Big Stan. He was working days because Big Stan heard about him pressuring free blow jobs off the girls at night. Not that Big Stan begrudged that service to anyone so long as they paid. Taz knocking off freebies was bad business.

"What's so important?" Taz said, lounging back against the pleather upholstery. The air inside the room was rich with the stink of disinfectant from a recent cleaning.

"I want to move on somebody. I need two more guys. You and a guy like you," Jerry said.

"Like me how?"

"Like you. Like big. Like somebody that can fuck a guy up."

Taz nodded, eyes half-lidded. Guilty as charged.

"I'm serious. This is real payday," Jerry said.

"How real?" Taz said.

"This guy just dropped ten kay in diamonds on my Uncle Danny. And that's what my uncle got for them. Probably closer to fifty kay retail. The guy has to have more."

"I know shit about diamonds." Taz's attention was waning.

"I'll move them. The guy is bound to have cash too. And he's all by himself. He's hiding from the police, I think."

"When?"

"Tomorrow maybe. I'll call you. Can you get another guy?"

"Sure. We splitting even?" Taz said, standing.

"Yeah."

"The diamonds too."

"Yeah, Taz. Trust me."

"Because if you fuck me you know what will happen," Taz said, parting the sequined curtain to depart.

"Yeah. You'll fuck me up," Jerry said, his sweating face parting in a nervous grin of what he hoped was fraternal ball-busting.

"Uh huh. And after I fuck you up I tell your uncle you fucked him and he'll fuck up what's left," Taz said as an adios and shifted through the curtains.

Jerry sank back into the tufted back of his chair and sighed. Then he straightened up, his hands leaping from the sticky pleather surface like fluttering birds. He imagined the genetic soup of fluids imbued into the furniture, carpet and walls of this place and shuddered. He practically leapt from the confines of the booth to charge past the dancer now slowly swaying, off tempo, to an old Spinners song. He was out of the lot, wheels spinning, back to the warehouse. He needed to be there to keep an eye on Uncle Danny and the Wasem brothers.

He wanted out of here. Out from under this uncle's thumb. Out from piss pots like Glitters. Out from running thankless errands for unimaginative men. And out of fucking Kansas.

By as soon as tomorrow night he'd be spreading wings for LA or Miami. Somewhere it wasn't cold. Somewhere where the only kind of snow you saw came lined up on a mirror at three hundred bucks a gram.

> Gunny Leffertz said:
> *"You walk into the lion's den you better expect there'll be lions. Only guy who had a fix in the lion's den was Daniel. Don't expect God to come bailing out your sorry ass."*

28

In his room at the Motel 8, Levon sorted the bills
from the gym bag. He made three piles atop the bed
covers. One was worn bills that had seen circulation.
Twenties and fifties. Another was lightly circulated
bills. All hundreds. The first and second piles were
from different series, different years, with varying
facility numbers.

The third pile was all crisp bills in fifty and one
hundred dollar denominations. They looked and felt
fresh from the mint even though the series marks
claimed they were almost twenty years old. Though
the serial numbers varied, they all bore the same
facility mark. The district numbers identified them
as coming out of Dallas. Those facts alone weren't
enough to cause suspicion. It was likely enough to
find newly minted bills together in a bundle straight
out of the Federal Reserve.

More troubling to Levon was the plate position
letter. This letter denotes where each individual bill
was situated when it came off the plate. Letters could
run from A1 to H4 on older bills. A1 to J5 on newer

ones. For this stack of bills to be genuine, one would have to accept an epic coincidence since each bill was marked with B3 for its plate position.

He'd seen bills like this before. In Tikrit. A room the size of a two-car garage concealed behind a false wall. Rows of plastic wrapped pallets stacked eight feet high — billions of dollars in bills much like the ones on the bed before him.

The suspect currency was all from the stacks he took from the vault back in Lake Bellevue. The rest were a mix of bills taken from the back room of the bar in Baltimore.

Levon put aside a little over one hundred thousand in bills from each of the three piles. He placed the remaining cash, a rough count of four hundred thousand, along with the envelopes of diamonds, in the gym bag and zipped it closed. He laced his sneakers, threw the gym bag over his shoulder and went for a run in the pre-dawn light.

* * *

The cell phone was jangling by the sink when Levon stepped from the steaming shower. He was back from a six mile run down the parkway and back.

It was Danny Safar.

"We have your goods. I'll send my guys over to you."

"There's a Chili's east of my hotel. I'll meet them in the parking lot in two hours."

"Two hours. If you have any more of those diamonds you need to move . . ."

"I don't."

"Two hours then," Safar said and broke off.

Levon dressed and packed the overnight bag with

everything in the room that he'd brought with him. He checked the room twice and left. He wouldn't be back.

A service road at the rear of the Motel 8 ran behind several other businesses fronted on the parkway joining one parking lot to another. Levon followed this. There was an open dumpster behind a Burger King.

The seating area outside the Starbucks offered a clear view of the parking lot of Chili's. He was an hour ahead of the meet time. Levon ordered a tall black coffee and sat alone at a table under an ice-crusted umbrella. The line of cars snaking around the building toward the drive-thru offered him cover while not obscuring his view. He could see the entire front lot and entry drive to the Chili's set well back from the road. He sipped the hot coffee and watched the lot through the blue haze of exhaust from the cars creeping past.

The wait wasn't long.

The same Mercury that picked him up two nights before pulled off the parkway onto the empty Chili's lot. The same woman was driving with the bearded Wasem brother in the front seat. The woman's head was bare, and her hair brushed back from her face. They drove around the Chili's twice before stopping in a slot at the rear of the restaurant.

They were thirty minutes early.

Both Wasems got out of the car and stood a while stamping their feet against the cold. They smoked and watched the lot. The woman sat behind the wheel of the running car, eyes wary, a cigarette hanging from her lips. The lean one spoke to the beard, gesturing toward the Starbucks. The beard trotted away from the Mercury toward where Levon was seated.

Levon hunched forward, head lowered to a USA Today, take-out cup to his mouth. The beard hustled into the Starbucks without noticing him. The store windows were misted over by condensation. Levon waited until the beard shouldered his way out with his hands full. Three tall cups and a pile of Danish in a cardboard tray.

Beard pulled up short when Levon turned to face him. He looked down at the steaming cups in his hands. Behind him, a couple of young guys were exiting the Starbucks, laughing at something one of them said.

"Tell them to come over here. The woman too. I'll take a table for us," Levon said.

Beard nodded and moved away as fast as he could manage without tipping the tray. The woman killed the motor and all three marched over to where Levon sat. The men took seats. The woman stood at the curb, smoking, with her back to them.

"You need to show more trust, friend," the lean one said with a crooked smile.

"Is that why you showed up early?" Levon said, his hands on the table either side of his cup.

"Mr. Safar wants you to know he has cash for you if you have more of that product," the lean one said.

"I made my deal. One time only. If Safar is happy then give me my stuff."

The lean one shrugged and opened his coat. Eyes locked on Levon, he slid a manila envelope onto the table.

Levon covered it with the newspaper and nodded to them.

"You're not going to look at it?" beard scoffed.

"I know where to find you if I'm not satisfied," Levon said, hands resting either side of the cup again.

"That burner we gave you. You got rid of that like Mr. Safar told you?" the lean one said, the smile faded now.

"Right before I came here," Levon lied.

"Then our business is done, right?" The lean one stood.

"Have a nice day, asshole," beard said in Arabic.

Levon watched them return to the car and drive off the lot onto the parkway before picking up the envelope folded inside the newspaper. He watched the lot a few minutes longer before leaving the table.

29

"Not so close. Hang back," Jerry said to Taz who was driving.

"You said not to lose him," Taz growled.

"He's walking, okay? Like he's not going to see this tank creeping along behind him," Jerry said.

They were in Taz's Yukon. A third guy, Jamil, was sprawled in the back seat with a pump shotgun in his lap. Jamil was not the bruiser Jerry imagined Taz would recruit. He had the look of a junkie, drawn face cratered with old acne scars. He was nicknamed Jamil, "handsome" because he wasn't. To Jerry, he looked like a hadji Keith Richards.

"Fuck it. I'll park and you watch him," Taz said and pulled to a stop on the shoulder in front of a Burger King.

They sat watching the white guy who called himself Dresher cross Parallel Parkway, trotting to beat the light turning yellow. The traffic closed behind him but Jerry could still see him. He was walking up the drive toward a Marriott Guest Quarters.

"Go, go!" Jerry said as the guy moved out of sight

behind some pines along the driveway.

They caught up to him just as he climbed into the back of a taxi from the queue lined up before the hotel entrance. Taz parked the Yukon along the curb.

"We'll hang back. Give him some room," Jerry said.

"You want to drive?" Taz said. A dry chuckle from the back seat.

"He's not carrying anything," Jerry said.

"Like what? Luggage?" Taz said.

"A bag. Something. Maybe he's going to get it."

"Maybe there is no bag. Maybe there's no diamonds, Jerry."

"Has to be. He's on the run, like I told you. You don't give up all your swag for eye-dee. And he bought the best. He's planning on vanishing for good. No one does that without holding back some goods."

The taxi swung out onto the parkway heading east toward the city. The Yukon followed, keeping two cars between them, pacing the taxi as just another car in the serpent of traffic hissing along the road wet with snowmelt.

* * *

In the rear of the taxi, Levon looked at the contents of the envelope. Everything he asked for was there and looked solid. To his practiced eye the licenses appeared flawless. The holograms were in register and the type perfect. Whoever did the work used Photoshop to vary his chin and the shape of his ears. Nothing noticeable to the casual observer but enough to avoid a match in any facial recog program should someone run it.

He paid more attention to the passport. The watermarks were in place. They even changed the colors of his shirt and the background in the photo. There were visa stamps showing that he'd visited the Dominican Republic. The paper was official. They'd either bleached a real passport using a laser process or found a source for blanks. These were fakes as good as any he'd seen from any intelligence agency. Better than some.

The cards and documents would need to be distressed a bit. The only weakness in them was that they looked too new. He could manage that when he got where he was going. He took one of the licenses and slid it into the window of his wallet along with the insurance card. The rest went back into the envelope and into the inside pocket of his coat.

He was Wayne Karl Lipscomb of Waco, Texas now. Merry's new name was Brittany Ann Lipscomb. Levon wasn't sure how she'd feel about that.

"This it?" the taxi driver said.

Levon looked through the salt-streaked window to see a neon sign for Dun-Deal Auto Sales coming up on the right.

"This is it," he said.

* * *

He got the salesman down to twelve thousand even on a '07 Toyota Tacoma. That was the amount he had set aside from his travel stash for the vehicle.

"You sure knew what you wanted," the salesman said, counting out the rumpled fifties and hundreds on his desktop.

"I drove around the lot when you were closed

Sunday," Levon lied.

"Well, you got a deal. We reconditioned her from bumper to bumper, Mr. Lipscomb," the salesmen said, stacking the bills in a tidy pile.

"Call me Wayne," Levon said with an open smile.

He was forty-five minutes from being dropped off to keys in hand. A new name for him and for Merry. He'd circle west through a few states before heading back toward Mississippi. Give it five days and he'd be able to pick up his little girl, sure he'd left a cold trail behind him.

* * *

"There he goes," Jerry Safar said, eyes gleaming red.

"I see him," Taz said allowing the bronze POS pickup and a couple more cars to pass them going west.

"He's going for the highway," Jerry said, eyes on the signs for the 70 on-ramps ahead.

"I see that too," Taz said.

"Change of plans. When he gets to some empty spot we can run him off the road," Jerry said.

"Fuck you. You want to do that cowboy shit you use your ride," Taz said in irritation as he swung them off the lot of Pep Boys in pursuit of the Toyota.

"So, you have a plan?" Jerry said, sullen.

"A plan." Jamil snickered in the back seat.

"Yeah. We see where he's going. If he goes too far, we take him when I say we take him," Taz said.

"When is that?"

"When I say. That's when."

"How long till then?" Jerry said.

"Jesus. You paying by the hour?" Taz said and pounded the wheel once with his fist.

Jamil giggled at that until it turned into a gurgling wheeze. Jerry slumped back in his seat and dug in his pocket for his smokes.

They fell in behind a black Camaro, all eyes on the Toyota with temp plates two cars ahead.

30

"Who doesn't have prints? I mean who has prints that don't show up anywhere?" Bill Marquez bitched to the dash mike as he drove. Rather, as he sat in beep and creep traffic on the beltway road around St. Louis. An icy drizzle was coming down. Just enough to bring the evening rush to a maddening crawl.

"Lots of people haven't been printed," Nancy Valdez said. Her voice came from the speakers on either side of him.

"Not guys like this. Not guys who act like this. Not guys who move this way. Did you see the surveillance?"

"I haven't seen anything but columns of numbers. They have us working the currency. We don't get to see the whole pyramid."

"The whole pyramid?" Bill asked.

"The pharaohs never let one crew build the whole pyramid. At least, not the interiors where the tombs were. Each crew worked separately so that no one crew knew the design of the whole thing," Nancy said. He heard her end her sentence with the distinct sound of parting lips and an exhalation.

"You're smoking again?"

"Caught me. This is boring work. They'll at least let me have twenty minutes for a ciggie break."

"Cold there?" he said with a smile she could hear.

"As a bitch."

"So, someone had to see the big picture, right? Some architect had to know how the whole pyramid came together."

"Sure. And when the work was done they cut out his tongue and blinded him. He knew but he couldn't tell anyone what he knew or even show them."

"Is that what they'd do to me?"

"Can you see the whole pyramid?"

"No. I'm either too close or too far away." Bill sighed. A school bus cut him off and a half dozen kids were at the back windows giving him the finger and laughing.

"The last hit on currency we got is what you had sent in from Carbondale. He paid for that train ticket with dirty money."

"Four days ago. He stopped using Blanco cash then."

"Or he wised up to which cash is on file. Or he's only spending in the underground economy. Those bills would take longer to get back to us. If they ever do."

"That's what I mean, Nance. This guy is on the run but he's not running. He's making very deliberate moves. First he divided us to chase him and the girl down dead ends. Then he vanishes like he was taken up to heaven. We have no known associates, no background and even our physical evidence lead to shit."

"Are we back to him being a member of the Maine crew?" Nancy said.

"That still makes no sense. Crews turn on each other all the time but not in the middle of the score." Bill's hands left the wheel to give the kids a double finger. They rolled away from the window laughing. Jesus, he thought, what are they? Eight? Nine?

"What do they have you doing then?"

"I'm running down stolen cars like a fresh-out-of-Quantico rookie. Do you know how many cars are boosted in St. Louis every day? I'm wondering if anyone here is driving their own car."

"Hey, I'm freezing. I have to get back inside," she said.

"Yeah. Good luck. You get anything I can use you'll ring, right?"

"Sure will. I want you back in DC," she said and broke the connection.

He finally crept up to his exit and eased down the ramp only to find the surface road he was trying to access backed up with a sea of flashing red lights.

The pyramid felt like it was getting farther and farther away, a distant mirage on the desert horizon.

31

He left the frozen white serpentine of the Missouri River behind him. The sky was a slate gray dome over the highway. The oncoming headlights, shining gem-like in the chill mist, grew fewer and farther between as he drove north.

Levon watched the Yukon in the rearview. He'd noticed it before turning north off 70 onto 435. It was hanging back, trying hard to look like it belonged. The thinning traffic of mostly long-haul trucks gave it scant few hiding places. The pursuer, if that's what it was, had no choice but to drop back, staying just ahead of the horizon line with twenty more miles to the next exit.

He dropped his speed to ten miles below the seventy-mile limit. The Yukon grew larger in the mirror before dropping its speed to match Levon's. An eighteen-wheeler blasted its horn as it swerved around the slowing vehicle. The big semi roared past Levon in the Tacoma leaving a storm of filthy spray in its wake.

Levon dropped his speed another ten miles,

moving now at a pokey fifty in the far right lane. The little pickup juddered like a ship at sea with the passing of each long-hauler. Most let him have a fanfare from their air horns loud enough to shimmy the glass in the doors. In the rearview he watched the Yukon close fast on him. Then it dropped back, left turn lights blinking yellow. He wasn't giving them a choice. They'd either have to ride his bumper or pass.

The Yukon leapt into the middle lane at the first gap that opened for it. In the side view now he watched the SUV cut off a big stack semi. It glided into the lane before the truck. The headlights of the semi-silhouetted the Yukon in its brights. Levon could see the shapes of two heads, a driver and a passenger.

He confirmed the headcount when the SUV rolled up to pass him on the left. He punched the gas to match the speed and allow the pursuing car to come even with him. Two men in the front seats. The back windows were almost black with road grime. He couldn't be sure there wasn't another passenger. The driver was a bald man, hunched over with fists on the wheel, fighting for position in the hammock position between the trucks rolling ahead and behind him. The passenger was sitting with his head fixed forward and unmoving as a crash test dummy.

Levon recognized him in any case. The go-fer from back at the Safar warehouse. Barry? Larry? Jerry.

The Yukon rolled past followed close by a truck riding on its back bumper. Levon let up on the gas to allow them to get out of sight over the rising road.

He removed the automatic from his waistband and laid it on the seat beside him.

* * *

"He made us," Jerry said.

"Made us?" Taz growled, head down over the wheel, eyes swiveling.

"He saw us."

"Then say that. You trying to sound like a cop on TV?"

Rhythmic snoring from the back seat. Jamil was asleep or nodding.

"We're going to need to take him alive," Jerry said, rummaging in his coat pockets.

"You making plans again?" Taz risked an angry glance at him.

"He's left town. He's got nothing on him. That means he hid his stash, right?"

"Back in K.C.?"

"Or maybe up ahead. Platte City or maybe up in Missouri."

"And after we take him alive?"

"We make him take us to his stash. Make him give it up," Jerry said, tipping powder from a tiny glass vial onto the web of his right hand.

"None of that shit in my car!" Taz shouted, leaning from the wheel to slap Jerry's hand from under his nose. A fine mist scattered, dusting the dash white.

"Damn, Taz! What the fuck?" Jerry wiped at the crystalline frost trapped in his mustache. He began to lick his fingers only to stop when Taz raised his open hand again.

"We need to be straight. Minds clear," Taz said,

giving Jerry a murderous look.

"Like him?" Jerry snorted, head bobbing to Jamil snoring behind them.

Taz grinned, revealing a row of gold molars. "He's okay. Heroin levels him out. That coke only makes you stupid. In your case, stupider."

"Yeah, okay," Jerry said with a sullen expression, wiping his hands on the leg of his jeans.

"We'll go with your plan. Take him alive. Happy now?" Taz said.

"Happy as shit," Jerry said, slumping down low in the seat, knees against the dash. He was watching in the side view at the lights of the Tacoma keeping a steady distance behind them.

He tried to light a cigarette only to have Taz reach over and pluck it from his mouth.

"No coke, no smoke in my ride," Taz said.

"Shit," Jerry groused and went back to his vigil in the mirror.

The Tacoma's lights were looming closer. The pickup was racing up on them, brights and hazards flashing.

"I see him," Taz said and punched the gas.

Jerry turned to look out the rear window. In the back seat, Jamil was still six fathoms under a heroin nod. The pickup rode their bumper close enough that Jerry could see the face of the guy at the wheel. The guy's face looked like it was carved from stone.

"What's he doing?" Jerry said.

"Fucking with us," Taz said, goosing them forward, building some distance.

The lights of the Toyota swerved away sharp to the right. Jerry watched in disgust as the little pickup roared up an off-ramp as the Yukon entered the shadow of an overpass.

Taz roared and hammered the wheel. Jamil woke up.

"It's fifteen miles to the next exit!" Jerry shouted.

"You want to go right out that door at seventy? Keep talking," Taz said, stabbing a finger at Jerry.

32

Levon had the Tacoma pulled up close to the pumps at a QuikTrip off 29 in Platte City. He saw the silvery dome of the canopy covering surveillance cameras mounted on the ceiling of the canopy over the pump island.

The Sig was on his seat pinned under his thigh. He leaned out the open window to press the call button on the stanchion below a symbol of a wheelchair.

A tinny female voice came from the speaker above the button. "Yeah. Help you?"

"Hey, I'm handicapped. Can I get a little help pumping gas?" Levon said.

"Sure. Hold on." The voice was kinder now.

A man hobbled out to the pump island, shrugging into a raincoat as he came.

"You need help, sir?" A kid. Twenty or twenty-one maybe, with the eyes of an older man.

"Could you fill it up? Regular."

The kid undid the cap and started the nozzle. He stepped back to Levon as the numbers whirred by on the pump.

"Iraq or Afghanistan?" the kid said.

"Excuse me?" Levon said.

"Where'd you get fucked up? You have the look. I apologize if I'm wrong," the kid said.

"Iraq. Anbar. Hurts like hell when it's cold like this."

"Tell me about it," the kid said, smiling easily as he lifted his pant leg to show the gleaming steel of a prosthetic above the top of his work boot.

"Still hurts sometimes even though it's not there anymore," the kid added with a crooked grin.

"An IED for me. What about you?" Levon said.

The kid shrugged. "Land mine. Or so they tell me. I don't remember anything about that day."

The nozzle clunked as the tank reached capacity. The kid replaced the nozzle on the pump face.

"Thirty-two fifty," the kid said.

Levon pressed a wad of bills into his hand. He could see the corners of two twenties.

"We're good. All right?"

"Sure. Take care, brother," the kid said as the Tacoma pulled out from under the canopy into the rain-snow mix coming down steady from a dark sky.

Back in the warmth of the QuikTrip he unfolded the wad. A hundred bucks in crumpled bills.

* * *

Levon paid for a car wash. He fed bills into the pay box on a stanchion before the entrance of the wash shed. He pulled in and waited in the steaming dark. The windows cleared, thin rivulets of water freezing over on the glass as the cold crept back in.

He remained parked when the wash was over and

the light turned green. He ignored the invitation and remained in the dark. No one else would be wanting a car wash in this downpour. Open panels along the walls of the shed offered a clear view of the south-bound ramp off the highway. Anyone coming off would have to slow for a light at the end of the ramp. He'd see them when they came back looking for him.

A thirty-mile round trip from the next exit north back to here. He used the time to get burgers and a Coke at a McDonald's just off the ramp before pull-ing into the car wash. He ate a burger and watched the ramp. Truck traffic rumbled by on the interstate, rushing past unseen on the floor of the trough.

Just under the half-hour mark the Yukon exited the highway and came to a stop at the light at the top of the ramp. Levon watched it make a right onto the surface road. He gave it time to get out of sight before pulling out of the wash to follow.

The Yukon was rolling slow past businesses lining the roadway. Levon pulled into the lot before a shuttered ice cream stand and cut his lights. The Yukon picked up speed once it was past the stores. He waited until the Yukon was out of sight in the gloom. He followed with lights out.

Houses were set well off the road either side. They sat on wooded lots. The trees thinned as the road rose between snow-covered fields lying fallow off the shoulders. Far off on the horizon he could see the top of a grain silo. Other than that and the sagging barbed wire fence running along the roadway, there were no other visible signs of humanity. The sky was low over the horizon as night came early. The rain was turning to a fine sleet that pelted the windshield.

The beads of ice hammered on the uninsulated cab roof over his head.

He topped the crest of the hill to find the Yukon parked on the shoulder off the oncoming lane, lights blinking. It had made a U-turn somewhere ahead.

Levon stomped the accelerator and jerked the wheel left. He locked the brakes and the truck hydroplaned sideways. He steered into it bringing the Tacoma to a hard stop against the side of the Yukon. A shower of safety glass flew in at him from his door window. He raised the Sig and fired three rounds through the jagged opening. All three took the passenger in the torso and head. The man flopped against the far door in a crimson spray.

Rolling out of the cab on the passenger side, Levon moved fast around the vehicles with the pistol raised in his fists. Nuggets of ice crunched under his boots. He swept the front seat of the Yukon with eyes over the front sights. The man in the passenger seat was unmoving. Jerry Safar leaned forward in the shoulder straps. Steam rose from the splash of gore spread over the dash.

He brought the Sig up to cover the dead fields. A man hobbled away over fallow prairie grass. Broad shoulders working, legs pumping, he leapt humps of frozen prairie grass. Levon raised sights and set his shoulders. He trained the front tangs center mass on the figure charging away into the graying dusk.

A click and squeal behind him. Levon turned at a motion from the Yukon. A man, a third man, was sitting up on the rear seat. A shotgun in his fists.

Levon felt an impact on his chest that slammed his lungs empty. He stumbled back toward the fence posts. His feet went out from under him, his legs suddenly numb. Then everything was numb. The early winter twilight turned into a night of absolute black.

33

"You have a lot of books," Merry said, running her
fingers along the spines of volumes lined neatly on
a wall of shelves in the cabin's great room.

"I do at that," Gunny said from the broad kitchen
table where he was making peanut butter and raisin
sandwiches for them both.

"Are they in braille?" she asked, pulling one down.

"A few. Most aren't." He held the jar of Skippy and
dipped the butter knife into it.

"How do you read them?"

"Oh, Joyce reads them to me if I ask her. I used to
get audiobooks but I like Joyce's voice better."

Merry thought about that a moment before walking to the table where she watched Gunny glide the
knife across the bread making a perfectly even smear
of peanut butter across each slice.

"Do you have a lot of books because you were a
teacher?" she asked.

"Now who told you I was a teacher?"

"Joyce said you taught my daddy. She said you
were a teacher at a very special school."

"I was," he said, sprinkling raisins to stick fast to the tacky smear of nut butter. "But nothing I taught Levon is in any of those books. Well, not all of it."

"Then where is it? What you taught my daddy?"

Gunny tapped a finger to his head and smiled at her.

"I don't understand," Merry said.

"You see, what I taught Levon, and other men taught him too, was the wealth of our experience. In the Marines we called it 'lessons learned.' You know what that means?"

Merry shook her head then remembered and said, "Unh-uh."

"Like when you stick your hand in a fire and get burned. That's a lesson learned. Fire burns. It hurts. You don't ever forget that. Someone could tell you over and over not to stick your hand in the fire but until you do it yourself you haven't really taken it to heart. Well, in the Marines we'd make mistakes and men would get hurt. Each time that was a lesson learned. Learned hard. Learned at a price. And so that other Marines didn't make the same mistake we'd share our experience with them."

"What kind of school was it?"

"It was called SERE."

"Sear?"

"It's letters that stand for Survival, Escape, Resistance, and Evasion. It was made to teach men like your father how to make it through tough times and tough situations. How to beat the odds."

"Did he do good in school?" she asked.

"Honey, your daddy was the best I ever saw. No matter how tough, how damned near impossible we made the tests, he passed every one. By the end he was teaching us. I never saw anyone like your daddy and that is the God's honest truth."

"What were the tests like?"

"That's something you better ask your daddy."

"Joyce told me you'd say that," Merry said.

"Well, she's right, honey. Now get the milk out of the fridge and pour us both a glass." Gunny slid her a plate with her sandwich, cut into four equal quarters, across the table to her.

Gunny Leffertz said:
"*Before they went three and oh with the Germans, the French were the badasses of Europe. The baddest of all those French badasses was Marshal Ney. He was Napoleon's favorite general. When the invasion of Russia turned into a clusterfuck, Ney volunteered to cover the retreat. My man was the last Frenchman out of Moscow. And I mean the last one. Months went by without a word from Ney as the French army froze and bled and died on their way out of Russia. Old Napoleon figured his boy was dead. Then one day Ney shows up at Napoleon's tent, covered head to toe in blood. And you know what he says to the little corporal? 'Don't worry. None of this blood is mine.'*"

34

He smelled blood as he came around. His nostrils
were full of the stink.

Levon opened his eyes to see Jerry Safar's face
inches from his. What was left of his face. One eye
stared at him, swollen with blood from an eight-ball
hemorrhage, lips pulled taut over yellow teeth. The
right side of his head was open in an obscene bloom
of bone and tissue created by the exit wound.

The floor shuddered under him. He was in the
rear cargo area of the Yukon. Knees up to his chest
in a fetal position. He tried to move and couldn't. His
hands were secured tight behind him. Plastic straps
that cut into the skin. Tie-wraps. His feet were bare;
ankles bound the same way. They'd taken his coat,
shirt and belt. He was in a Henley shirt and jeans.
His chest hurt with each breath. He shifted himself,
bringing fresh pain. He wasn't bleeding. As far as
he could tell, his ribs were bruised but intact. All
the blood was from the corpse, drying sticky in the
grooves of the plastic floor mat.

A voice was coming from somewhere up front.

One half of a conversation. Someone on a phone.

"I don't know how he'll handle it. It's his nephew, you know? It's all fucked up."

Pause.

"If you say so, boss. If you could handle it for us. Tell us what to do."

Pause.

"Yeah. We're an hour away. You want us to go straight there?"

Pause.

"Uh huh. Jamil bean-bagged him. Fucked him up good."

Pause.

"I don't know who the fuck he is. A white guy. He bought new eye-dee off of Danny Safar. Good stuff. Jerry said it cost twenty kay. The guy paid in cut diamonds. That's why we were dogging him."

Pause.

"He didn't have any stones on him. Only cash."

Pause.

"A hundred kay abouts. Fifties. Hundreds."

Pause.

"Okay. Okay. We'll bring him there. Thanks, boss."

Levon heard the muted beep as the connection was broken.

"Are we fucked?" A new voice. Raspy. Laconic. Closer to Levon. The speaker was in the back seat. The man with the shotgun. The man he'd missed.

"I don't think so. Stan says we're cool. Says Danny didn't have much use for Jerry anyway."

"They say that now."

"Stan wouldn't fuck us."

"You think that?" A gurgling chuckle.

"He gets half what we took off this guy. Gives half of that to Safar. That smooths things over."

"What do we do with the guy?"

"He goes to the red house. Stan'll decide what to do with him."

"And Jerry?"

"Stan says that's our problem."

"Shit."

"You can say 'shit,' but it's my car that's fucked. And half of fifty kay doesn't cover me for that."

They kept talking. Levon pressed the soles of his feet to the wall and pushed to help him sit up. The pain in his chest lanced deeper. The man in the back seat had hit him with a beanbag round fired from a shotgun. Blunt force delivered at ballistic speed. Only his thick clothing saved him from caved-in ribs.

His feet were getting numb, pins and needles. His fingers too. His arms pinned under him. He had to get his weight off of them. He levered himself up for a better view out the rear window. He flexed feet and hands to restore circulation.

Freezing rain crept across the tinted windows in fractal patterns. The lights of trucks glared through the wet glass making kaleidoscope reflections. The Yukon was on the highway heading back to Kansas City. The speaker said they were an hour out.

Levon bunched and worked his muscles, forcing blood into them. He shifted his bound hands under him. There was some give but not much. He might be able to get them under his rump and work them down his legs to get his hands in front of him. It would hurt but he could manage it if he kept flexible, worked at it slow and steady.

He shifted his weight and the tie-wrap on his wrist scraped against a channel in the floor mat, popping against the plastic lip of the groove.

A face appeared over the back seat. Gaunt and drawn. Dead eyes that narrowed when they met his. The man made a clucking sound, scolding Levon like a child.

The man reached over the seat. An iridescent blue blaze in his eyes and the sharp rasp in his ears of a stun gun. Those were Levon's last sensations.

35

Sonata slept most of the time. The other girls talked or watched the television in the big room they shared. Sonata sought the escape of sleep and only woke for meals.

She dreamed of sunny days and walks in the park in Riga. She was a little girl in the dreams. She held her grandmother's hand until they reached the big field in the middle of the park. Then her grandmother would release her hand and she would run over the grass pretending she was a wild pony or maybe a fairy soaring low over the buttercups and clover. Always in the dreams, she was a little girl, a child in the days before she knew the world as she knew it now.

They told the girls that they would be moving soon. That soon they would go to rich American husbands. Sonata did not believe that. She did not think any of the girls did. Even the ones who said they did believe it.

It could not be true. She knew though she said nothing to the others. If it were true, then they would be preparing them for their new husbands. Most of the girls were still in the same filthy clothes they'd come here in. Some needed to see dentists. One girl had a severe cough that got worse every day. Sonata saw blood in the sputum the girl left on the floor.

They lied to themselves and talked to one another about their futures in America. The first few days they watched the television in wonder. They could not understand a word of what they heard but what they saw was a rich country where even the poor were fat and everyone had big houses and cars.

A favorite channel of the girls had shows where young couples looked for a house to live in. The couples never seemed to go to work and would act like princes and princesses while the hosts practically begged them to spend their money on houses that were always beautiful. The show would end with a party in which the young couple would have their friends over to see their new home. They lived lives without worries or cares and never anything to fear.

The men who worked in the house regarded the girls the way they might rabbits in a cage. Three men watched over the house. They had guns they wore on belts under their shirts. There was always two of them here. Only one at a time would leave on one errand or another. Usually, it was to bring back greasy prepared food for the girls. Sandwiches and sodas. Sometimes pizza or pasta. Cheap food. Nothing fresh.

One man would leave and another would make certain the door was locked behind him. The windows were locked and barred and covered in heavy drapes. Some of the panes were painted with a thin coat of paint that let in only muted light.

In the upstairs bedroom she shared with five other girls, Sonata scraped a tiny circle in the paint through which she looked out through the bars to see sunlight. The view was limited. The bare branches of trees growing close. Cars moving on a faraway street beyond the trees. During the day the sun flashed off windshields. At night the headlights were points of drifting radiance. She imagined they were boats moving on a canal.

There was a fourth man who came to the house sometimes. His name was Kola. He smiled all the time and liked talking to the girls. For this reason Sonata feared him. She preferred to be ignored. She did everything to make herself seem small when Kola was around. She did not speak. She moved, trying not to seem as though she intended to, to be as far from Kola as she could.

Kola would make jokes and the girls would laugh. He knew enough languages to make himself understood to most of them. Latvian. Serb. Ukrainian. He had sex with some of the girls. They went outside with him sometimes. Some were eager to do so in the hope that he would favor them in some way. Others were less willing but went with him anyway. They had been broken long before. Drugged and raped on the boat that had brought them here. Their will was not their own. Kola would take a girl's hand and lead her out into the cold air. The girl would smile. Sonata would see their eyes. They were the eyes of a doll. The smile of a doll. All life gone.

Some of the women came back with stories of having sex in the back of Kola's car. They would come back with gifts of candy and cigarettes. They would tell the others of Kola's big car. White upholstery with heated seats. A big American car like on the television.

There were other girls who came back less giddy at being chosen. One girl, a Serb with a mane of red hair, came back in the house bleeding from the mouth. An angry bruise encircled one of her wrists. The next day the side of her face puffed up, purple flesh stretched over broken skin. Her eyes were black all around with a smeared veil of mascara. The girls asked what she had done to deserve such treatment. The redhead said nothing.

The next day, one of the men found her on the bathroom floor. She'd slit her arms with a piece of broken mirror. They told all the girls to go to their rooms. Sonata watched through her peephole in the glass while two of the men carried the redhead away wrapped in a shower curtain. The plastic leaked a scarlet trail on the snow all the way to a car parked out front. They stuffed her in the trunk and one of them drove the car away.

"You want to go outside?" Vanya said. She was one of the girls who shared the room with Sonata.

"What?" Sonata said, dropping the heavy drape back in place.

"You are always looking outside. I see you," Vanya said.

"Don't you want to go outside?"

"I do go out. With Kola. He takes me to his car." Vanya was one of the girls who accepted Kola's invitations with keenness. She would walk to the door beaming like Cinderella, celebrating the moment as if he might not have chosen any of the others over her. And on most occasions did.

"I don't want to do that. I do not like Kola."

"You don't have to like him, little one." Vanya laughed. "You just go to his car and suck his cock. He gives you gifts for it. Maybe he would let you go for a walk in the snow. Hm?"

"Leave me alone," Sonata said and turned away to the wall.

"Go to sleep then, little one. When you wake up it will still be the same shitty world." Vanya huffed and left the room.

Sleeping so much distorted Sonata's sense of time. Often she would be sleepless at night, lying wide awake listening to the sounds of the house. The girls gently breathing in the other beds. The muted sound of the television downstairs, their guards watching their own programs.

Very late one night, Sonata heard the sounds of tires on snow. She slipped from bed and stooped to spy through the scrape in the paint, the drapes closed behind her.

A big blue car pulled close enough to the house that she could not see it past the roof below. Voices rose from downstairs. She crept to the bedroom door in time to hear the bolts on the front door being shot back. Voices below. They spoke English. Men she did not know were here.

She felt a thrill of fear that set her legs trembling. Strange men meant something bad to her. They came to take the girls away. Or maybe they were here on a visit like Kola, to use the girls any way they wished. Maybe they were worse than Kola. Like the men on the boat.

Before she realized what she was doing she had entered the hallway and rushed over the carpeted floor for the bathroom. They couldn't have her if they couldn't find her. The tile was cold under her bare feet. She pushed the door closed, but left a gap in case they heard the snick of the lock below. She sat on the floor against the wall by the door, watching the hallway.

Sonata had no ideas for an escape from the house. The mad inspiration that made her seek a hiding place was pure animal flight. No plan. No greater aspiration than to hide as long as she could to forestall the men from finding her. The giddy thought raced through her mind that they might take the other girls and leave her behind, forgotten.

The voices came closer. The fluorescent lights in the hallway ceiling blinked on. Sonata shrank back. Feet on the stairs. Men grunting.

Through the narrow gap she watched two men carrying a third between them. The man they carried was a big man and the two men struggled with the weight. His hands and feet were tied together. A dead weight. Unconscious.

One of the guards led them to a room at the end of the hall. It was a bedroom that no one used. It was water damaged from a leak in the roof. The wallpaper was gray and moldy. A black stain spread across the ceiling.

The three men went into the room. They spoke in English, muffled. There was some scuffling. One of them cursed. Then they were in the hall again and moved past Sonata's view to return downstairs. The hall went dark. After a while the sounds of a football game from the television rose again.

Sonata slipped back to her bed. She lay watching the ceiling until it was washed pink with dawn light.

36

Jamil lay against the curb, arms spread, staring upward. Snowflakes rested on the surface of his wide open eyes. They did not melt — Jamil's body temperature had reached freezing point hours before. Snow stood on the rest of his naked flesh.

He seemed to be regarding the pair of K.C. homicide detectives who were bent to study him.

"Junkie."

"What was your first clue, Sherlock?"

"Look at the tracks on his arms. Bet we find more in his crotch."

"You can find more in his crotch."

"Got all the pictures you need?" one of the homicide bulls said to the crime scene tech taking photos.

The tech nodded.

"Get him to the M.E. Send us a report," one bull said, holding up the yellow tape for his partner to duck under.

The M.E. determined that Muhammed Faiez Isa, AKA Jamil, died of an overdose of an opiate derivative. His fingerprints identified him as a felon with a record going back to shortly after he reached eighteen and right up to a year ago when he served six months for aggravated assault.

But it wasn't as simple as another junkie overdose.

Barbara Triplet had been a Wyandotte County medical examiner for ten years. Sometimes she regretted not following her one-time plan of being a dentist. Then she'd weigh the pros and cons of a decade of cutting on corpses against staring into people's open mouths five days a week. It always came out even. And this job had the bonus of patients who wouldn't try to talk while she worked.

She stood by Jamil lying on the table and read off the details of the tox screen to an assistant named Kyle who typed it all onto a laptop. Medical Examiners didn't recite their findings into a microphone anymore. It all had to be entered into forms. Boxes filled in and number codes provided.

"Any additional notes for homicide?" Kyle asked, eyes on the screen.

"Explain why there was a delay. We had to wait until his blood thawed enough to make the draw," Barbara said, leaning over the staring corpse. He wore an expression of dismayed surprise. An ugly guy even when he was alive. He'd been frozen like a Popsicle Christ when they brought him, arms spread with rigor and the cold.

"This guy came into money recently," Barbara said.

"Yeah?" Kyle said with only mild interest. No curiosity, these kids.

"I've seen it before. Longtime junkie gets a windfall. Now he can afford the good stuff. But he's not used to it and plows a week's worth of hits into his arm all at once."

"Maybe he won the lottery." Kyle snorted.

"You laugh, but there was this guy down in Florida? Won the Powerball. He could buy primo pharma quality smack now. Held big parties at his brand new redneck mansion. All the drugs you could want laying out like a buffet at an Italian wedding. Killed off most of his friends O.D.ing on the best dope of their lives. He died himself a year later. Same way."

"So, unintentional suicide," Kyle said.

"Not so fast, padawan. There are complications. He was found flat on his back. But livor mortis is all along his right side. He laid a while that way after he was dead. Someone moved him, dumped him. That's foul play. Even if someone didn't mean to kill him, they transported his corpse. Felony time."

"Didn't want him found at their house," Kyle said, tapping into the laptop: decedent moved from the location of demise by persons unknown.

"Or place of business. But, hey, we're not paid to be detectives," Barbara said. "Finish the forms and send them over to homicide. Make sure you get the names right on the leads. And make a note that I have additional physical evidence I'm bagging and entering."

That would have been the end of it. One more junkie no one would miss. Only this junkie had a mother who had a K.C. city councilman for a brother who promised to rain all kinds of shit down on Kansas City PD and the Wyandotte County sheriff if the people who murdered his nephew weren't brought to justice. And that's how it bounced back to homicide as a legitimate murder investigation.

"Goddamn Arabs stick together," one of the bulls

said.

"I think he was a Turk," the other said.

"Fuck's the difference. They're all a pain in my ass."

The detectives' shared line of reasoning mirrored that of the M.E. The junkie died somewhere inconvenient and needed to be moved. Best bet was a place of business. An illegal business. There were two hot-sheet motels within two miles of where the junkie was dumped. And one cathouse inside the same radius.

They operated on the theory that their stiff would go with the cathouse. The tox screen said he was loaded to the hairline with medical grade morphine, the champagne of opiates. That cost him. It fell in line with a windfall.

"If you've got the cash why not go where there's premium pussy?" As one of the bulls put it.

The house in the middle of the fourteen hundred block of Calvin Street was called Barbie's Playhouse by local vice. It was an upscale operation, at least compared to picking up tweakers and trannies down on Independence Avenue. The girls were as clean as their last HIV test and they were all females with their original God-given parts. In the right light some of them might even be called pretty.

It was an operation ultimately run by "Big Stan" Stomata, a Turk who owned a chain of car washes, four Arby's and two strip clubs in addition to the house on Calvin and various other holdings. He was connected with the city by campaign contributions and was a player in all the right charitable organizations. Big Stan had juice but not as much juice as the city councilman. That meant the only courtesy Big

Stan rated was a phone call before the two homicide bulls arrived with a half dozen uniforms for back-up.

They didn't need the back-up. The daytime manager met them on the front walk and escorted them inside, all smiles. The bulls pulled on vinyl gloves and did a casual walk-through of the premises. They peeked into rooms decorated like cheap Halloween versions of Victorian boudoirs, Chinese throne rooms, Roman villas and even a dungeon in the basement. In the light of day it all looked tacky as hell. But to the customers, fueled by hormones and alcohol, they might look like Hollywood sets.

The girls, three who were on daytime stand-by for walk-ins, sat in the living room watching reality TV and doing each other's nails. They could be sorority sisters but for the hard eyes and cheap dye jobs.

"I like it," said one bull after the survey.

"I like it too," said the other.

They informed the day manager that they were shutting him down until a crime scene unit went over the place.

"You have a warrant, right?" the day manager said. No animosity. It wasn't a challenge. He only wanted to make sure the protocols were followed in case his boss asked.

"Here's your copy, chief," one of the bulls said and held a three sheet form out to the manager.

"What are you looking for?" The manager held the form close to make certain the address was listed correctly.

"Carpet fibers," the other bull said.

"Carpet fibers?" the manager said.

"Yeah. Science. Fuck yeah," the bull said.

Gunny Leffertz said:

"You need to live in the now. Right now. Fuck the future. The future is fear. Fuck fear. We don't do fear."

37

They started with a beating.

That let him know they'd done this before.

They knew not to start by asking questions.

First, supremacy must be established. The subject must be shown that the interrogator is in charge. The subject must learn that his will is not his own. He belongs to his interrogator. There is no hope and no respite coming. Mercy is a quality unheard of unless the subject does something to earn it. And only the interrogator can determine the price for clemency.

He was naked. They'd cut off his clothes and taken them away. He had only a thin blanket to cover him against the cold. That was torn away when the single ceiling light came on and the room filled with strange men.

Levon curled up as much as he could on the narrow bed, the only piece of furniture in the tiny room. He protected his head. He tensed his muscles against the blows.

Two big men. One to hold him down, a knee on

his neck. The other punched him in the torso in a workmanlike fashion. Thorough.

Gut.

Flanks.

Lower back.

Thorough but not professional. They were bouncers or brawlers. They could tune a guy up to collect money. Teach a hard lesson over a slight. Prison yard bullying.

The blows to his already-bruised ribs pained him the most. His side was a map of dark blue flesh. He let them know it hurt with grunts and gasps. They didn't want to kill him and laid off the ribcage at the order of a third man leaning in the doorway watching.

The third guy was smaller than the other two but clearly calling the shots. Slight build, sallow skin. A mop of badly dyed blond hair. A cigarette clamped in the corner of a permanent sneer of derision. The guy barked and the two heavies let up on Levon. They panted from the effort. The room filled with their beer sweat.

Listening, Levon lay still on the bare mattress, moaning for their benefit. The shot-caller spoke, hustling the heavies from the room. A language Levon was familiar with but wasn't fluent in. Turkish, maybe. The lights went out. The door was shut. A whiff of foreign tobacco in the air.

He reached to catch the corner of the blanket in his fingers. He did his best to pull it over him. Staying warm was key. He allowed his muscles to relax then tensed them again. Legs, arms, shoulders, hips. Working blood into protesting limbs, fighting the stiffness that would cripple him when he needed to move.

They'd beat him again. Maybe one or two more times. Then the shot-caller would get down to business. The questions would start.

From there it was a balancing act. They wanted the money and the diamonds they were sure he was hiding. They'd found his get money in his clothes. It was enough to shake up the men who brought him down, enough for them to hand him up to their masters. Now he was in the hands of men only interested in what he could give them. And once they were convinced that he was a vessel they could empty at will they'd expect him to pay off.

Levon would allow them to think he was broken when it suited his goals. And his only goal was to escape. And to accomplish that he'd have to allow them to hurt him. But not hurt him enough to impede his escape. That meant playing the hand he was dealt and playing it on his timetable not theirs.

He contracted and released his muscles and stretched his joints as best he could while he surveyed the room again. The shadows of the window frame on the floor told him it was late afternoon. The window faced west. It was barred on the outside and nailed shut on the inside. The panes were too narrow for him to squeeze through even if he broke the glass. His cell was a room in an older home. There was no closet. A hundred-year-old house. The only door led to a hallway. The door was solid wood in a wooden frame. No deadbolt. No lock of any kind that he could see. The knob was a cut-glass antique.

They'd offered him no food of any kind or any water to drink. His internal clock told him that it was more than twenty-four hours since his last meal. He could go another forty-eight before that presented a problem. And he'd gone longer and still remained ambulatory.

He considered more immediate options. He was limber enough and had enough strength to work his bound wrists over his ass and down his legs until he had his hands in front of him. Only that would be of no use to him with his ankles still wrapped tight in plastic strips. With his hands, even bound, before him and his legs free he could make the rest work to his advantage. The room offered nothing that would allow him to cut through the plastic. Nothing that would let him do it quickly in any case.

There was no telling when his captors would return. If they caught him halfway through working his hands to the front or sawing through his bonds with the edge of a piece of glass it would go hard for him. He'd be bound even tighter and probably after a vindictive beatdown.

The only bright spot was that they had not secured him to the steel frame bed. He still had the range of motion his bindings allowed him. He could get off the bed if only in a pathetic hop.

He took that cold comfort with him as he willed himself to sleep, the last restorative alternative left to him.

* * *

It was dark in the room, nighttime dark, when the three men returned for another beating. This time they dragged him to the floor to work at him with kicks.

When it was over they made to go. Levon chose his words carefully, choking them out in wet sobs.

"Please. Please. What do you want?"

A snicker from the blond. The room went dark. The door closed with a click.

> Gunny Leffertz said:
> *"When the shit is rising and the piss is raining down you remember that you are not alone. Jesus is with you and I am with you. And even after Jesus runs away calling for his mommy, I will still be there with you. And you dare not fucking give up on me. Give up on yourself. Give up on our country. But give up on me and I will fuck you up here and in heaven."*

38

The door opened again.

It was still the same night, he was sure of it.

Levon lay where they'd left him on the bare wooden floor with his back to the door.

A slender bar of light lay over him. He could hear an intake of breath behind him.

A woman.

He rolled over to see a girl peeping in at him. Her dark eyes were wide. Her mouth parted in surprise. She was petite with narrow shoulders and slender arms and legs. Dark hair fell to her shoulders. Her eyes darted to the side at a noise from somewhere deeper in the house. She reached for the knob to pull the door closed again.

"Can you help me?" he said, voice low, just for her to hear.

Her fingers rested on the doorknob. She said something in a whisper — a question. Something in the language sounded Slavic. Soft consonants. Elongated vowel sounds.

"I am hungry," Levon said, trying Russian.

She blinked and stared, pupils darkening. She understood.

"Please. I am hungry and thirsty," he said.

The girl nodded and slowly pulled the door closed.

He watched the bar of yellow light beneath the door. The muted sounds of a television somewhere. Voices talking merrily. The music of a commercial that he remembered only because Merry laughed each time she saw it. The scent of cigarette smoke.

A shadow appeared in the strip of light. The door opened and the girl entered, pressing the door shut behind her without a sound. She knelt by his side and set something on the floor before helping him to a sitting position.

"For you to drink," she said in inexpert Russian.

He felt a can touch his lips — some kind of soda. Her hand gently cradled his head, she tipped the can enough to let him slurp mouthfuls of the sweet stuff. He drank steadily until the can was empty. He could see her smiling at him in the gloom. A child's smile beneath dispirited eyes.

"Thank you. You are an angel," he said as she pulled the can away, resting back on her heels. She turned her head, the smile gone, her eyes cast down.

"Can you help me?" he asked.

"I am nobody," she said, voice small.

"Can you help me?"

"I am nobody," she said, soft as vespers.

"My name is Levon," he said.

She said nothing.

"I have a little girl of my own." Reaching out. Making a connection. Touching her somehow.

Her eyes were closed now.

"A little girl like you."

She spoke, a whisper. He strained to hear.

"Not like me. Not like me," she said.

The ceiling lamp came on bathing them both in pitiless light.

39

After days without a new lead the task force was falling apart.

Homeland was peeling away agents and officers, reassigning them to serve a system that was already overwhelmed. With the results of their labor showing less and less promise, the local and state cops were offering more excuses than help.

Bill Marquez was down to one Tom. Agent Doolin was called to the Chicago office. That left him and Agent Salucci as the total company of Team Roeder. They were working and reworking the threads of evidence left for them in St. Louis.

Down in Memphis, Team Megan had already been rolled up. The trail of the little girl and her mysterious female guardian went stone cold. The video from the train station was of no help. The unknown woman with the serious skills never turned her face to any of the eight cameras covering the station interior. She was Caucasian with short cut hair. Five foot seven inches. One hundred and ten to one hundred and thirty pounds. Hard to pin down because she was wearing winter clothes. Military or law enforcement background probable. Exterior cameras didn't even catch what vehicle the pair left in. If any.

Bill had access to interagency databases and other resources but had nothing new to feed them. It was four days and no sparks rose to meet him. Deputy Director Wysocki, who no longer insisted on being called "Darren", was pressing harder even as he shrank Bill's army to a force of two.

"I'm a little stretched here, sir," Bill said during their scheduled three o'clock call.

"Get me some fresh meat and I can send manpower your way. But the only thing worse than two agents playing with themselves is a dozen agents playing with themselves," Wysocki said by way of a sign-off.

The three o'clock call was over by three-oh-four.

Bill and the remaining Tom split up. Salucci went to re-question and re-re-question witnesses at the airport. Bill sat in a stuffy little office the local bureau had loaned him. He reviewed video surveillance until he wasn't even sure what he was looking for. He studied Tex's every move until he was sure he'd recognized the man in silhouette if he ever spotted him. After binge-watching the same footage over and over it became clear that this guy wanted to be seen at St. Louis airport. He wanted them to waste time following leads drawing them down a rabbit hole. He made them spread their efforts in all the wrong directions. Mission accomplished.

His phone buzzed, waking him up. Bill had dropped off watching a loop of the suspect moving across a concourse entrance in full view of the TSA cameras.

It was Nancy Valdez.

"Thought I'd give you a heads-up before you heard it officially," she said.

"You got another hit? Bills from the Maine score?" Bill said, rubbing a fist in his eye.

"Oh yeah. But even better than hot serial numbers." He could hear the grin in her voice. Pictured her freckled nose crinkling.

"Yeah?"

"How about counterfeits? Righteous ones. Prime phonies. Over ten kay in hundreds and fifties that would fool anybody but our techs."

"Where'd this happen?" Bill said.

"Kansas City, Kansas. Local cops were searching a whorehouse on an unrelated matter and uncovered the bundle. Scans of a few of the bills just came in. This place lit up like Christmas."

"And they're part of the Blanco stash?"

"The years are right. Bills from 1998 and '99. They bear all the signatures of being run off in Iraq. Part of the billions Saddam Hussein produced back then. And that points back to Courtland Blanco. He did business with Iraq during the sanctions."

"Jesus," Bill said, sipping the sweet acid of coffee long gone cold.

"Your case just got shit-hot again. This fairy story about billions in hidden assets got real," she said.

His phone bonged in his ear. Call waiting. He made his apologies. She wished him happy hunting and got off.

It was Wysocki ordering him to K.C. Flying this time. Military transport. Wheels up in sixty.

40

"What is your name, you filthy whore? Who told you could go in there?"

Kola dragged Sonata away from the room where the naked man lay on the floor. Even over Kola's ugly words she could hear the sound of flesh on flesh as the two big men beat the naked man. Kola jerked her by the wrist toward the stairs. She yanked back on his arm, trying to break the grip, bare feet skidding on the carpet.

He turned back to her and drove a fist into her face. The force of the blow dropped her to the floor. She tasted blood in her mouth. His rings cut the flesh of her cheek. She lay at his feet, vision swimming in swirling shades of red and white.

Kola stood over her and called back to the men. The dull thuds ceased within the room. They stepped into the hall. One of them sucked at blood streaming from a split knuckle.

"You may have ruined everything, bitch. Why do you do that?" Kola was crouched over her, shrieking.

"He was thirsty," she said.

"Bitch," he said between his teeth, blowing foul smoke in her face.

"I am sorry," she said, looking away.

"What is your name?"

"Sonata." Her eyes on the floor.

"Like the car?" He brayed, amused.

Like the song, she was about to say before he pulled her to her feet, a fist tight in the hair at the back of her head.

"I will show you my car, okay?" He guided her before him like a puppet, her toes skipping along the floor as if in flight.

She did not understand his words until they were down the stairs and heading out the front door into the cold and dark.

* * *

It was punishment this time. All sense of purpose was gone. No method. Only anger.

One of the men held him on his feet, wrists pulled up behind him. The other slammed his right fist over and over into his face. Levon rocked his head back with each blow, anticipating it. He bent his knees to take the impact. That brought a wrench upwards from the man holding him that threatened to rip ligaments in his shoulders. His teeth tore the inside of his cheeks. Blood spewed from his mouth with the next blow.

A shout from the hallway. The hands holding his wrists pulled away. Off balance, Levon fell to the floor. The lights went out. The door slammed in its frame. There were screams from outside the room. They grew louder even as the source withdrew. Then they were cut off and the house was silent again but for the distant television sounds.

Levon lay on his side trying to fix his eyes on an invisible horizon. The room was spinning. It was jerking right to left, right to left like something was trying to shake him off the carpet. He fought the urge to close his eyes. That would only make vertigo worse. He needed to stay conscious.

In his mind he heard Gunny Leffertz' voice. It rang loud and clear and direct.

"You stay with me, asshole! I did not dismiss you! I did not tell you that you could go anywhere, pogue! You dare not close your eyes on me! I am not tired yet! Do you understand me?"

"Yes," Levon whispered, spraying blood.

"Did I hear you say something, pogue? Did you say something?"

"Yes," Levon said again louder.

"I've heard pussy farts louder than that! Let me hear you, pogue!"

"Yes!"

"You are never leaving this room," Gunny said softly, his voice coming inches from Levon's ear.

The hell I'm not, Levon thought, eyes fixed on that invisible horizon, willing it to stay level for one second. Just one second and he could hold on.

The second passed like an hour.

The world went gray.

Then black.

Then nothing.

Gunny Leffertz said:
"They have you. Really have you. You're going to talk. They'll know if you're lying so you can't lie. The only

*tactic you have left is to hold back the
truth until it does you the most good
and them the least. You have what they
want. Hold onto it as long as you can."*

41

The next time they came they came wanting him to talk.

The last beating moved up his timeline. Another one like it and they might break a bone or blind him. That would complicate his escape plans.

The vertigo has subsided but was still there. He felt as if he was floating on a surface of shifting liquid. He tamped down the sensation before it could rise to engulf him.

Two big guys, one Levon hadn't seen before now, lifted him from the floor and held him upright for the blond-dye job.

"This is not fun for me," the blond called Kola said. Levon picked the name out from exchanges he'd overheard.

"This is work. Do not make it harder work, okay? You give to me. I give to you." Kola took Levon's chin in his hand.

Levon nodded, eyes lowered. Submitting, telling his captor that he was surrendering control.

"Is there more money? More diamonds? I think

there is," Kola said, face close to Levon's. Stale cigarettes and garlic on his breath.

Levon nodded.

"Tell me where and I give you water. Or a soda
maybe. Order you a pizza."

Levon swallowed. His eyes darting as though in
desperate thought.

"Do not lie to me. Do not make hard work for
me."

"I won't lie. I've had enough." Levon raised his
eyes to look into Kola's.

Kola gave his cheek a playful slap.

"Tell me."

Levon described the location of the gym bag in
detail. Kola entered the location on a smartphone.
He looked up at Levon with hard eyes.

"I will be back. If you are lying to me, making up
stories, then I will make you hurt. Hurt for a long
time." Kola gestured to the men holding him.

"Haluk, you come with me."

Levon was dropped to the floor. The men left
the room. Morning light came through the dirty
window.

Kola broke one of the primary rules of interrogation. He broke his promise to give Levon water
in exchange for information. The broken contract
confirmed what Levon knew already: once Kola and
his masters had what they wanted they would kill
him.

He had an hour until Kola got back with the bag.
Less if Kola phoned to confirm he had it when he
found it. And he would find it. Levon had told him
the truth of the bag's location. It was the fastest way
to get himself and the bag in the same location.

Levon rolled onto his knees and got his bound feet under him. From there he rose to a standing position. He dropped into a deep crouch, bending his legs, balancing on his toes. He hunched his shoulders forward then back, folding his torso at the same time. The pain in his ribs was a burning spear in his side. His abdominal muscles, bruised deep from the beatings, protested as he tightened them. Within seconds he was running with sweat despite the cold. He blew his lungs empty of air.

Bent double to make as small a silhouette as possible, he worked his bound fists under his ass. The plastic cord cut deep into the flesh of his wrists as he pulled the flex-tie to its fullest length. He worked the inch or two of slack under him until his hands were under his legs. He unbent his legs slowly as he slid his hands down to his knees. Then dropped down to a sitting position, bound feet lifted, and slid the binding free until he had his hands before him at last.

He rolled to the bed and levered himself up to lean on the footboard. Rather than tying his wrists with a single wrap, someone had used three bands. Two flex-ties acted as cuffs on each wrist, linked by a third looped through the cuffs and drawn tight to bring his wrists together. His ankles were bound the same way. One tie he could break, bringing his wrists down against his hip, straining the plastic locking mechanism until it broke open. This current configuration made that impossible.

Levon got his shoulder under a corner of the mattress and raised it up until the edge of the metal frame was exposed. He began sawing the band between his wrists back and forth along the top of the side panel. The edge was rounded but pitted with corrosion creating enough of an edge to bite into the plastic. He ran the connecting cuff across it. Blood ran from cuts on his wrists. They cut deeper as he pulled the band taut. Rust came away from the metal with each slide along the edge. He could feel the plastic strap begin to give a little. Another minute or two of work and he'd be free.

Across the room, the glass knob turned and the door opened.

It was Sonata, her face purple with bruises.

In her hand she held a kitchen knife with a long serrated edge.

42

The federal search warrant was good. The address correctly spelled. The list of suspect items described in minute detail. After a call from DHS a judge signed off on it in record time. It was legal perfection, flawless and unassailable.

And about two hours too late.

The cathouse on Calvin Street gave them a starting place. Carpet fibers found on an overdosed addict matched the flooring in one of the rooms. In the search for the carpet fibers the cops found, and confiscated as evidence all belongings they found that related to the deceased including clothing, key ring, and a suspiciously empty wallet. Suggestions of a call to Immigration brought two of the self-described sex workers to Jesus. They handed over the cash they'd looted off the corpse before management had his naked ass hauled away. It was a pimp roll close to ten kay in bills that looked righteous enough. Except the homicide bulls agreed that they didn't like the odds of finding that many bills of 1990's mintage all in one spot.

Looking into the background of the dead junkie turned up a W-9 tax form claiming that Muhammed Faiez Isa was employed as a security guard by Well-Dun Entertainment Enterprises. The bulls knew that to also be an operation owned by Seyfettin Ahmet Stomata. Big Stan.

So, the dead junkie was working off a little employee discount at the Calvin Street house.

The day manager allowed that he remembered knowing the deceased after all. The junkie worked part-time as a bouncer at Glitters, one of two strip bars owned by Big Stan in K.C. on the Kansas side.

This was all getting too deep and too wide for the homicide bulls. Both were pleased when scans of the fishy Benjamins came back from Treasury marked for a hold. The feds were on the phone to K.C Homicide in minutes and in their faces inside an hour.

FBI and ATF teamed for the search of Glitters, and just to be certain, Silky's, Big Stan's other "gentleman's establishment" in town. They were looking for more of Saddam's awesome counterfeits. The managers of each place complied with the warrants but the agents found not one suspect bill in the safes or registers at either bar.

In fact, the office safes in both places were suspiciously empty of anything beyond property tax records and papers relating to liquor and entertainment licenses. No money or checks of any kind. And, as the raids had taken place before noon, there weren't even dancers on the clock — not even a glance of a naked tit for all their trouble.

"They knew we were coming," Bill Marquez said, staring into the bereft safe in the back room office of Glitters. The team at Silky's had already radioed that there was no joy there either.

"Of course they did. The local cops turned over a rock when they busted that whorehouse. You can't keep that kind of news locked down," Tom Salucci said, kicking at a mess of spilled papers on the floor. Feds were not tidy searchers.

"This money means that the dead junkie encountered our runner somewhere," Bill said.

"Okay." Salucci shrugged.

"And the junkie got a bundle of cash off our guy. And even the dumbest junkie in the world knows he can't keep that kind of bundle to himself for long."

"Sure. Stands to reason."

"They'd pay up to whoever runs their crew. The top guy. Give him a taste. But these safes are bare. Two all-cash businesses and there's no cash."

Salucci waggled his fingers to urge Bill on.

"So that gives us an opening to run down all the other businesses associated with Stomata in order to find the rest of the suspect cash. I bet we turn up our runner in one of those places. He paid this money for a reason. To provide a hide-out or maybe to get himself smuggled out of the country."

"That's a stretch, Bill. A judge isn't going to buy throwing a net that wide based on that theory. Weak stuff, I hate to tell you."

"Wysocki can sell it. He can sell it to a judge. He can sell it up the line," Bill said, stopping to pick up a handful of papers spilled from a file.

"You think so? How?" Salucci said.

Bill shook the papers in Salucci's face like a tambourine. A feral leer on his face. The face of a predator smelling blood.

"Because you shake this Turkish treehouse hard enough and a bushel load of Mohammeds and Achmeds are bound to drop out."

43

Kola drove past Schlitterbahn on his left, keeping his Lincoln in the right-hand lane.

"He said it's up here ahead," he said to Haluk in the passenger seat. Haluk nodded.

A bead of lights moved by on the interstate. The span created deep shadows beneath. The Lincoln slowed and pulled onto the shoulder in the sheltering dark, moving slow. Kola leaned across the seat to look at the understructure of the overpass. A car horn honked as the traffic hissed by.

"There," Kola said, bringing the car to a stop.

Haluk nodded.

"See the ladder? He said there's a bag up there at the top." Kola pointed at the rusting hoops set in the berm rising from the surface road to a cave-like opening in the dark above.

Haluk nodded again, slowly.

"Get your ass up there and look," Kola growled.

Haluk grunted and opened the door to lift his bulk out and onto the gravel. Kola sat in the warm interior of the Town Car and watched through the sunroof. The big man climbed the rungs up the concrete slope to the top. Haluk moved slowly at first but picked up a rhythm. He soon vanished into the gloom above. He was gone only a few minutes. Kola watched the mirrors for cop cars. Only one, a county sheriff's car, buzzed past without slowing. Not to say they might not circle around and come back.

"Come on, esek," he muttered to himself over and over like a prayer.

Haluk's big ass swung into view high atop the berm. He was moving with dainty steps as he climbed backwards down the rungs to the road surface. Kola spied the gym bag slung over the man's shoulder and the breath caught in his throat.

Kola leaned across the console to swing the passenger door open. Breathing hard, Haluk bundled himself inside, the bag on his lap. Kola gunned the car off the shoulder, spraying gravel, and into traffic.

Further along the parkway, they pulled onto the lot of a Waffle House. Kola took the bag onto his lap and unzipped it.

"Sik beni." Fuck me, Kola sighed at the heap of bundled cash inside the bag. He looked over to see Haluk's eyes wide, a wolf's leer growing on his face. Kola zipped the bag closed and tossed it in the back seat.

"Call Savas. Tell him to take care of things at the house," Kola said, turning the car on the lot to take them back out onto Parallel Parkway.

Haluk fished a cell from the pocket of his coat and poked the keys with his gorilla fingers. He held the phone to his ear, blinking.

"He's not answering," Haluk said.

Gunny Leffertz said:

*"The ground at your back is only safe
if everyone there is dead."*

44

Savas did not hear the man approach. In an instant, an arm was about his neck, closing on his throat with a suffocating pressure, pressing him back into the chair with irresistible force. The arm was naked and smeared with drying blood. A fist clasped about the wrist of the choking arm, cinching the noose tighter.

He clawed for the gun in the waistband at the small of his back but only succeeded in trapping his hand against the chair back. With his free hand he clawed at the arm encircling his neck. He dug his nails into the hard flesh, drawing fresh blood. The arm would not yield. If anything the terrible hold increased in force. He looked to the girls seated in chairs and on sofas all around him in the great room. Savas opened his mouth to plead for help. No sound emerged.

The girls turned from the television to regard him. He saw some of them look past him to the man applying the deadly pressure to his neck. They watched with the same level of attention they showed for the hours and hours of television they watched. After a few seconds most decided that the telenovela they were watching held more interest and they turned away.

Somewhere through the fading rhythm of his pulse he heard a high trilling sound. On the coffee table before him his cell phone came alight and danced in place. He released his grip on the choking arm to reach out, fingers splayed and quivering for the cell. Leaning forward only increased the strangling pressure.

A feminine hand picked up the cell from the table. It was the mousy little Latvian. Her battered face creased in a tiny smile. Her eyes, hooded by swollen flesh, watched him with animal ferocity. His gaze locked on those dark eyes, staring at him from twin caves of bruised tissue.

Savas jerked in spasms. Fought for air. Fought to remain conscious. His heels ground furrows in the carpet. He pissed himself. Then, like the moon passing behind clouds, those damning eyes boring into his vanished behind a curtain of black.

* * *

"He is dead," Sonata said.

"Not yet," Levon said between gritted teeth, keeping the choke hold tight. He had a knee jammed into the seat back. Sweat stood on his skin with the effort. A crimson slick ran down his arms and back. He could feel the big man's weakening pulse through his biceps. He waited until it flickered away to nothing then counted thirty before releasing.

"What does the phone say?" Levon shoved the man in the chair forward. He pulled a .38 in a heavy frame from a clamshell holster in the corpse's waistband.

"Haluk. He was another one of the men who watched us," Sonata said.

"Is he the one with Kola?"

"Yes."

"That's all the guards then?" Levon found a ring of keys in the dead man's pocket. It included a key remote and ignition key for a Mustang.

Sonata nodded, thinking of the man called Yafuz lying on the kitchen floor in a spreading pool of blood. The naked man took him down in total silence, striking over and over again with the knife she gave him, striking with lightning speed to the soft tissue of Yafuz's underarm, driving the long blade deep into the heart and lungs. A hand clasped tight over the big man's mouth and nose. All over in seconds while Sonata watched in dumb wonder.

Then the naked man she freed drained a quart of milk he found in the refrigerator.

"If they called that means they're thirty minutes out," Levon said. He snapped his fingers in her face. Sonata lifted her eyes from the black-faced man slumped motionless in the chair.

Some of the girls, certain now that something in their world had changed, rose from their seats. Exchanging glances and whispers they drifted away and up the stairs to their rooms.

"We leave?" Sonata said.

"I need clothes. Do the men keep clothes here?" Levon said.

"They have a room where they sleep sometimes." She nodded toward the back of the house.

"Let's go," he said and followed the girl, the .38 in one fist and a Czech 9mm, taken off the man in the kitchen, in the other. The key remote was in his teeth.

The back room looked like it might have been servant's quarters at one time. There was a twin bed and dresser. Some shirts and socks in the drawers. A sweatshirt and sweat pants lay discarded on a chair.

"Wait here," Levon said and stepped into a bathroom. A steel tub rimed with rust with a new shower nozzle hooked up to the faucet. He squatted in the tub and ran steaming hot water over himself. The floor of the tub turned crimson. Lifting his head back, he drank some of the warm water raining down on him. He cleaned the wounds to his wrists and ankles with a bar of soap. He dried himself with the cleanest towel he could find. Then he tore the towel into strips. He wrapped his wrists and tied them tight.

Sonata was sitting on the bed waiting for him. A sweat suit, t-shirt and socks lay beside her.

"Do you have warm clothes for yourself? Winter clothes?" he asked as he dressed.

She shook her head.

"Well, put on whatever clothes you have and meet me in the living room. Layer them. You understand?"

"Put on many clothes?"

"That's right. Put on many clothes," he said. She ran from the room.

He could hear her bare feet rushing up the stairs as he laced a pair of Nikes he found under the bed. With an extra pair of socks on his feet they were close enough to his size. There was a fleece-lined jacket on the back of the door. He took it with him to the living room. He turned off the lights all around the room. He muted the TV but left it on. The flickering light created a strobing effect on the room. A digital home fire.

Sonata rushed down the steps wearing a sweater two sizes too big over a white blouse and jeans. On her feet were some boat shoes more suited to summer at the beach. She wore thick wool socks under them. The ensemble managed to make her look even more petite than she was, a little girl playing dress-up. The illusion was dispelled when she brushed her hair back to reveal swelling that distorted her face.

"You'll need this too," Levon said and handed her the fleece-lined jacket. He moved to stand by a front window, parting one of the heavy drapes to watch the driveway before the house. He could see the late model Mustang parked in the shadows. He keyed the remote once. The car's lights flashed yellow.

"We are leaving? You will take me with you?" she said, draping the jacket over her shoulders.

"I will. But first we're going to wait for my money to come back," Levon said.

45

"You understand I'm well outside of my jurisdiction?" the Kansas State trooper said from behind the wheel of an unmarked state car. The blue light atop it cleared the lanes ahead, currents of red lights parting to allow them through.

"As of when?" Bill Marquez asked.

"As of the middle of the Heart of America bridge a minute or so back. We're on the Missouri side now," the trooper said.

"Looks like more Kansas to me," Tom Salucci said from the back seat, watching the rooftops of warehouses blur past.

"We need your help finding this place. We'll say you're with us. Assisting federal agents in pursuit of a suspect," Bill said. The trooper was not much reassured by this.

"You can wear one of our windbreakers," Salucci said, amused by the young trooper's discomfort.

"Very generous of you," the trooper said and pushed the unmarked harder down the highway following the signs for Raytown.

"I wanted to keep this sweep under as tight a wraps as we could manage, okay? This Stomata organization already has a hair up its ass and there are more rocks to turn over. The three-hour delay on the warrants didn't help," Bill told the trooper.

"We're looking for counterfeit cash?" the trooper asked.

"That's what it says on the warrants. But Tom and I think that the money is long gone, hidden where we'll never find it or destroyed by now," Bill said.

"Then what are we looking for?"

"A white male. Six foot plus. Lean. I have pictures on my phone. He's on the terror watch list," Bill said.

It was an exaggeration. They couldn't put someone on the watch list until they had at least a tentative ID. There were no John Does on the list. The man in the pictures from St. Louis airport was still a ghost, a nameless perpetrator that existed only as a digital image.

Wysocki at DHS had weaved a tale of smoke and mirrors for a magistrate judge to issue a warrant. The suspect list on the warrant was peppered with names that sounded like probable candidates for ISIS membership. That made it all go down easier. The fact was that the closest this bunch of Turks got to honoring Allah was watering the drinks at their strip joints. If the feds found their man all would be excused. The guy had roamed across a dozen states killing everyone he met. Nailing him for terrorism should be cake. Deputy Director Wysocki might even let Bill start calling him "Darren" again.

But first they had to find Tex, AKA Roeder, AKA Dresher.

Other units of combined federal agents and state cops spent the evening tossing dry cleaners, used car dealerships, laundromats, bars and fast food places all owned jointly under the umbrella of Nu-Seff Enterprises Incorporated in Nevada. The name was derived from a combination of Seyfettin Stomata and his wife Nuray. On paper she was a full partner though Bill doubted she was aware of this.

Bill and Salucci joined in a few of the more likely raids at the bars and clubs, turning up nada. Bill had no stomach for terrorizing laundromat managers or shaking used car salesmen out of bed. And he didn't expect to find their runner hiding in a tumble dryer or the trunk of a creampuff Cadillac. Bill scanned the list of Nu-Seff holdings for something that smelled right. Or, more accurately, smelled wrong.

He landed on a property in a residential area of Raytown, a suburb of K.C., Missouri that had been slipping out of the middle class since the turn of the millennium. Googling the address convinced him that this long hunch might pay off. The map showed a rambling house sitting well back on a wooded lot at the end of a cul de sac. Of all the other addresses on the list, this one looked most likely to be a bolt hole for old Tex. It reminded Bill of a Bugs Bunny cartoon he'd seen as a kid. A gangster's getaway destination had a blinking neon sign on the roof announcing in six-foot-high letters that it was a HIDE-OUT.

The unmarked veered off for an exit marked East 63rd Street.

"How much farther?" Bill asked.

"Ten minutes out," the trooper said.

"Kill the lights. We go in quiet," Bill said.

From the back seat came the spung, spung, spung sound of Salucci checking the load in a pump shotgun.

46

Levon caught the men exiting the Lincoln Town Car. They were at their most vulnerable and unsuspecting then. When they stepped from either side of the car he keyed the remote for the Mustang, setting off the car alarm.

Both men turned at the bleating horn and flashing lights. Levon stepped from the shadows in front of the house, firing the Czech pistol to bring down first the one called Kola and next to his beefy companion. Emptying the pistol as he closed on them he walked across the yard. When the action locked back he tossed it aside.

With the snub nose .38 he finished off the larger man Haluk with two head shots. The big man's feet kicked at the snow twice and then were still.

Levon stepped around the car. Kola lay on his back feebly attempting to unbutton his coat with palsied fingers. He wheezed wetly from a half dozen shots to his chest. The man had a look of profound confusion frozen on his face. That look faded to a gaze into the infinite a half second before Levon opened his skull with a double tap.

Sonata was beside Levon and made to spit on Kola's still form. Levon clapped a hand over her mouth.

"DNA," he said.

She nodded, not really understanding, swallowing her spit, and he lowered his hand.

"Get the bag out of their car," he told her.

Levon crouched and removed his own Sig Sauer from under Kola's coat. He checked the load in the Sig and dropped the .38 to the snow. On the bigger man he found a Taurus automatic .45 with a spare magazine. Sonata came to him with the gym bag, a fragile smile on her face.

"Your money?" she said.

He nodded. "My money."

From somewhere beyond the trees he could hear the sound of an approaching car. Headlights glowed on the approach street.

Levon took Sonata's hand and pulled her into the dark away from the house.

47

Bill Marquez was out of the unmarked before it came to a full stop. His gun was in his fist though he didn't recall drawing it. He charged toward the dark house with the red clapboard siding, ignoring Salucci calling out to him.

Two bodies lay on either side of a Lincoln. Doors open. The snow a pink slush beneath them.

"Back up! Radio for back up!" Tom Salucci shouted to the statie before running to follow his partner. The statie, his shotgun cradled in his arms, turned back to his car.

Bill shouldered the front door open and bawled out a warning as he swept the front room with his sights.

"Federal agents! Ef! Bee! Eye!"

Salucci crashed in behind him, the shotgun held high and traversing to the right to cover the opening to a shadowed dining room.

A still figure sat slumped deeply in an armchair in the flickering light of the silent big screen.

"Federal agents! We're serving a warrant!" Bill

bellowed to the empty room as he made his way to the bottom of the stairs.

Panicked squeals and footfalls from the floor above.

"We're too late, Bill," Salucci said, backing toward him, the shotgun trained to cover their six.

"He's here. I know it. I feel it," Bill seethed through clenched teeth and started up the steps.

Gunshots from outside. Five shots in rapid succession. The boom of a twelve gauge.

Bill pushed past Salucci to race for the front door. The roar of a racing car engine and tires spitting gravel.

The statie was face down on the snow by the unmarked. His shotgun was gone. The front tires of the unmarked were shredded flat. Same for the Lincoln. The red tail lights of a car swerved away down the street.

The Mustang.

"Shit! Shit!" Bill hissed. He reached the open door of the unmarked to find the radio destroyed by a load of buck fired into the dash at point blank range. The Remington pump lay still smoking on the seat where the shooter had left it.

He knelt to touch the throat of the statie. He was breathing but had a nasty lump rising on the back of his close-shaven scalp.

Salucci was already on his cell calling it in. He gave their location and a description of the escape vehicle, such as it was. He reported an officer down and requested an ambulance.

Bill punched the glass of the unmarked hard enough to star it. He stooped to pick up a handful of snow to hold to his bruised knuckles. He looked up at the dark house and listened to Salucci giving directions to a K.C., Missouri police dispatcher. In the windows on the second floor he could see silhouettes cast against the glass.

The phone still to his ear, Salucci turned to him.

"Local PD are on their way and an ambulance. They're going to throw a ring around this place. We'll get him."

Bill turned away, shaking his head. The locals were stretched thin. The Mustang would be well away by the time any kind of effective roadblock could be set up. The rest of their task force was miles away on the wrong side of the Missouri River. It would be sheer luck if anyone spotted the runner based on the weak description of the escape vehicle. Mustang: unknown year. Color: dark. License number: unknown.

So far, the runner had luck on his side every step of the way. Bill had no real hope that his string of good fortune would end tonight.

48

Sonata stared in wonder at the contents of the bag open on the console between them. The rough man with the kind voice counted out bills from the bound stacks that filled the bag.

The sun was just becoming visible over the rooftops in a slate-colored sky. They were parked in the rear lot of a place called Howlin' Hounds Coffee in Omaha, Nebraska. They'd driven through the night to get here. Across a street was the Trailways bus terminal.

"There's fifty thousand here for you. Wait until you get where you're going to spend these, right?" he said, placing four thick stacks of twenties in her hand. They were wrapped in rubber bands.

"Fifty thousand dollars. Is that a lot of money here?" She goggled at the well-thumbed stacks.

"It's enough to give you a good start wherever you wind up," he said.

"I cannot go with you?"

"No. You'll forget you ever met me. That's all you owe me."

She nodded.

He handed her a smaller stack of very clean, crisp bills that looked new. "Use this money to buy your bus ticket to Cleveland, Ohio."

"Cleveland?"

"There's a bus leaving at nine-thirty. You'll be in Cleveland by tonight. You use this money to buy your ticket. The drug store is open. Buy anything you need there but use this cash, right?"

"Right."

"Any money from this stack that's left over you throw away in a trash bin before you get on the bus. You understand?"

"Throw away?" she said in disbelief.

"This is bad money. It's not real money. You don't want the government finding you, do you?"

She shook her head emphatically.

"There are a lot of Russians in Cleveland, Sonata. Find a church and ask them to help you."

She nodded, eyes welling with tears.

"You have three hours until the bus leaves. See the drug store over there?" He pointed at a Walgreen's on the corner across the street. Yellow light glowed from inside.

"They'll have stuff you need. Buy a bag for travel. A sweatshirt, toothbrush and all that. Stuff for breakfast. Use the bad money. You understand?"

"I understand." She snuffled.

"You'll be okay now, Sonata."

With a sob, she leapt over the console to hug him about the neck, holding him tight until he pried her thin arms from him. His neck was wet with her tears.

"Where are you going? Say it," he said, his hands still gentle on her arms.

"Cleve-uh-land. Oh hi yo," she said, eyes gleaming.

She stood on the lot and watched him pull onto an empty street and drive out of sight. She hugged the jacket he'd given her tight about her. The thick bundles of cash in the pockets were pressed against her belly. She shivered in the bitter wind blowing along Jones Street. The smell of hot coffee reached her and she turned, stomach rumbling, for the lights of the coffee shop.

49

"Spring is on the way," Gunny Leffertz said, his face raised to a beam of sunlight coming through the trees.

"All I see is snow," Merry said.

They were on their after-breakfast morning walk through the woods. Today they followed a game trail north. There was fresh sign that deer had come this way.

"You have to smell it, girl. Take a deep breath in through your nose. You can smell the trees coming back to life."

Merry sniffed the air until her sinuses stung with cold.

"I don't smell anything, Gunny."

"That's because your nose is dumb. Pretty but dumb."

They walked on farther, the cabin lost in the trees behind them. Merry led the way, watching ahead for the deer that had made the tracks visible on the trail. Gunny followed behind her, moving easily along the familiar trail he'd walked countless times. The old Marine walked with such a sure foot it was easy to forget he was sightless.

"Gunny," she whispered, cautious not to alert any deer that might be near, "spring is on the way."

"Do you smell it now?" he said in a hushed voice.

"I can see it," she said and knelt in the snow of a clearing where the green shoots of plants poked through the white cover.

"Crocuses? Thought I smelled them," he said with an open smile.

She squinted with skepticism as he stepped closer. "You smelled them?"

"They haven't bloomed yet, have they?" He crouched down by her.

"No."

"They'll be purple when they do."

"How do you know?" she said.

"They smell purple." He nodded gravely.

She giggled.

Gunny touched her arm and squeezed. His head canted.

"You hear something? The deer?" she asked, her voice low.

"Not deer. Something else." His blind eyes narrowed under a furrowed brow.

Merry listened too. She closed her eyes the way Gunny taught her and let the world in through her ears. The tiniest shift in sound ahead and to the left of the trail. A crunch of a boot sole on snow. The brush of cloth on cloth.

She opened her eyes to see her father standing among the trees watching her. A smile creased his face.

"Sorry. I think I scared the herd off," Levon said.

Merry raced to his arms and crushed herself against him, a smile on her face so big that it hurt.

50

The perky little redhead from the fifth floor stuck her head in his door for the eighth time that morning.

"This isn't going away," she said, all teeth.

"I only want you to go away," Brett Tsukuda said from his desk. He brushed at her in the vain hope that she might vanish.

"The Bureau. Treasury. They keep requesting background. Your silence speaks volumes." She was all the way into his office now.

"My silence screams itself hoarse." He lifted a coffee mug to his lips. Stone cold. He sipped it anyway in hopes the caffeine would take the edge off his migraine.

"And Homeland. They're worried about this hitting the news. I could warm that for you," she said and reached for the mug.

"Cold coffee is my penance. Can't you back them down? Does no one fear the NSA anymore?" He rubbed the heel of his hand into one eye until all he could see was white static.

"Not since we got our skirts dirty with PRISM.

Until then most American thought 'NSA' was a typo for NASA."

"What do they want from us?"

"Positive eye-dee on a guy they're calling AKA Mitchell Roeder for lack of a better option. They have fingerprints, high-res pictures and DNA. And they swear we know more than we're saying."

"Quantico passes on this?"

"They're pleading ignorance," she said and moved a stack of files from his guest chair to the floor. She plopped into the seat.

"Those papers were there for a reason," Brett said with a wince. Another gulp of cold hazelnut blend.

"Homeland is going to press the president," she said. "The director has a golf date with him tomorrow afternoon."

"If I'm lucky he'll have a good game and forget to call me."

"With his swing? He'll probably call you from the ninth green just to take his mind off his score."

"Yeah. I'm never that lucky," Brett said and tapped the sharkskin hilt of the tanto knife he used as a letter opener.

Her eyes were alight like a child expecting a bedtime story. "Who is this guy? Why can't we either bring him in or hand him up?"

"I must say, at the risk of being charged with insensitive remarks, that curiosity is unattractive on you."

"You're deflecting."

"Damn right I am. Look, give me until tee-off tomorrow to come up with something that works."

"Works for who? The agency? The country? This asset you're protecting?"

"Works for everyone, smartass," he said and shooed her with more vigor than before. She rose from the chair with reluctance, but paused at the door.

"I'll buzz you when Marine One is in the air," she said and departed.

Brett sat tapping the hilt of the tanto. He grimaced at his reflection in the dark monitor on his desk.

"Damn you, Cade," he growled, saying a name he'd vowed long ago never to speak aloud again.

A LOOK AT BOOK FIVE:
LEVON'S KIN

The fifth book in the dark, crime thriller series—Levon Cade.

On the run from the law, Levon Cade and his daughter Merry head back to the hills and hollers that Levon once called home. But his return opens old wounds and tears brand new ones when a man from his past involves him in a deadly game.

A gang war erupts in the high country, with Levon and those he loves caught in the crossfire. A massacre in the deep woods leads to an underworld manhunt for those responsible. Soon, the scenic mountain roads are awash in blood as the body count rises.

His back to the wall, Levon is not about to back down or give up ground...because this time it's family.

COMING MARCH 2022

ABOUT THE AUTHOR

Born and raised in Philadelphia, Chuck Dixon worked a variety of jobs from driving an ice cream truck to working graveyard at a 7-11 before trying his hand as a writer. After a brief sojourn in children's books he turned to his childhood love of comic books. In his thirty years as a writer for Marvel, DC Comics and other publishers, Chuck built a reputation as a prolific and versatile freelancer working on a wide variety titles and genres from Conan the Barbarian to SpongeBob SquarePants. His graphic novel adaptation of J.R.R. Tolkien's The Hobbit continues to be an international bestseller translated into fifty languages. He is the co-creator (with Graham Nolan) of the Batman villain Bane, the first enduring member added to the Dark Knight's rogue's gallery in forty years. He was also one of the seminal writers responsible for the continuing popularity of Marvel Comics' The Punisher.

After making his name in comics, Chuck moved to prose in 2011 and has since written over twenty novels, mostly in the action-thriller genre with a few side-trips to horror, hardboiled noir and western. The transition from the comics form to prose has been a life-altering event for him. As Chuck says, "writing a comic is like getting on a roller coaster while writing a novel is more like a long car trip with a bunch of people you'll learn to hate." His Levon Cade novels are currently in production as a television series from Sylvester Stallone's Balboa Productions. He currently lives in central Florida and, no, he does not miss the snow.

CPSIA information can be obtained
at www.ICGtesting.com
Printed in the USA
LVHW101916030222
710169LV00019B/2069